I0538270

Suited and Tied

By

Mungoni Manoge

© PJ NTSOANE

Give a Read Gift

© PJ NTSOANE
PO Box 941
Lebowakgomo
0737

© All rights reserved. No part of this publication may be reproduced, stored in retrieval system, or transmitted in any form or by any means, electronic, mechanical, photocopying, recording, or otherwise without either the prior written permission of the publishers or license permitting restricted copying.

ISBN: 978-0-620-58158-5

Cover design by Marcus and Lope

This book is dedicated to my lovely children.

Mungoni Manoge

About the author

*Mungoni Manoge is a pen name used by Photoane Jeffrey
Ntsoane. The name echoes the name of his tribe Bakone ba
Manoge who are part of the baKone (baKoni) tribes found in
the northern parts of the Republic of South Africa. Oral history
says that they are the same family as the amaNguni in
Southern Africa and Angoni in Central Africa.*
NB: *Mungoni Manoge is opposed to tribalism, racism and
gender discrimination.*

About the book
*This book satirizes patriarchy which unfairly discriminates
against women. It shows the paradox of development generated
by globalisation and African value system. This novel is set in
the African countryside where governance dominated by men
displays flaws exploited by unscrupulous investors from the
East. The fabric of modern African society is explored through
the hardships faced by a young woman who is a victim of
discriminatory practices and crime.*
NB: *This book is fiction. Names used in this novel do not bear
any reference to individuals or places in the real world.*

©PJ Ntsoane

1

It is a hot and humid Saturday afternoon in the African countryside where a sprawling village of Motsetona is located. Men are arriving in dribs and drabs at the royal homestead where numerous cases brought by villagers are heard almost on a daily basis.

Today's case is a delicate one as it involves a woman who is at loggerheads with her in-laws. The young Malesedi is a career woman whose husband passed away in the past few weeks. Women are only allowed to attend court sessions as plaintiffs or respondents. They are expected to have their heads covered. When they talk they are not allowed to stand up or lift their faces to look at the audience. Malesedi's in-laws demand that she should mourn her husband's passing in a traditional way. This is contrary to her religious belief. The elders of her in-laws have had several deliberations with Malesedi's parents without any success. They have ultimately reported the matter to Chief Kgoratau of Motsetona village since he has jurisdiction. He is a stern patriarch who regards himself as a custodian of his ancestral culture. He has married ten wives himself. Malesedi is a university graduate with a Master's degree in Sociology. Her elders from the neighbouring tribe are also expected to attend. Now the Royal Court Yard of Motsetona village is buzzing with men of different

©PJ Ntsoane

shapes and sizes who are wiping downpours of sweat from their faces. All of them are wearing jackets as no man is allowed to enter the royal court without it. There are some who are wearing expensive tuxedos. These are the ones who have been to the big city or have children who work there. Those who claim to be wearing the best shoes often dust them to make them shinier. Whenever they talk you notice occasional downward glancing in an attempt to draw your attention to the expensive leather.

There is deep murmuring and occasional coughs coupled with a roar of laughter. Where men are gathered, there is likelihood of hearing swipes as they try to cut one another down to size. They boast to one another about clothes, shoes, cars, women, children, sports, and even the sizes of their clubs. There is an African saying that, '*Masogana ga a rwešane dihlora*' - loosely translated it means: 'Young men do not crown each other'. A typical African man always has an insatiable penchant for blowing his own horn. Here is one of the stories that would make men roll with laughter whenever they are narrated:
There was this bulky guy who used to boast that he wielded the biggest club in the village. It was rumoured that one day while on a hunting exercise with a group of friends, he stumbled upon a sleeping rabbit. He was so

©PJ Ntsoane

excited since the group members had made a bet that whoever got the first kill without the help of the others could keep it all. This guy felt it was his lucky day since he had never killed any wild animal before. His foot was so close to the rabbit that he didn't want to reposition himself or make any unnecessary movement that would rouse the rabbit lest it escaped. It is said that he could have merely picked it up, but that would have bungled a heroic kill and his friends' envy. He held his club tightly in his hand, aimed, and unleashed a deadly blow with all his might. Other group members were only alerted by a loud groan of anguish. He had mysteriously missed the rabbit but managed to hit his own foot. Several of his toes were broken. The hunting expedition had to be abandoned because he had to be carried to hospital. He became a joke of the village. Men would tease him and say: 'It is not the size of the club that matters but the skill in using it'. Some rubbed it in by saying that even an old woman could have done a better job on that day.

While those who gathered there in the Royal Court yard were waiting to form a traditional quorum and the arrival of the royal elders who were always late, Sekele, a man who was renowned for his incessant fabricated stories cleared his throat and nudged Lekala, a middle aged man who was sitting next to him.

©PJ Ntsoane

"What is the matter now, Sekele? Can't you sit still?" asked Lekala, clutching his ribs feeling the pain inflicted by Sekele.

"You know what? I have something to share with you my friend," he retorted.

"I know you Sekele, you have started with your diabolical lies," said Lekala.

"No, this is the truth my friend, I promise you. I swear on my grandmother's grave," said Sekele reassuringly.

"Okay then, what is it?" asked Lekala.

"You know, some people are ungrateful," he said.

"Who did what now?" asked Lekala.

"It was my neighbour, Sakago. Last night when I was at home I heard a loud banging on his gate. It was a sound often made by people who wanted to draw the attention of those at home whenever they found the gate locked. My neighbour's son is the one who usually comes home late after partying the night away. I thought it was him as I recognised his voice. What really made me curious and my hair to stand on edge was a loud cry that followed the loud crash of the gate. I looked outside and saw that the gate had fallen and it seemed to have trapped someone. I immediately rushed out to investigate and help. When I came closer I heard a faint cry of anguish beneath the fallen gate," he shook his head and cursed.

©PJ Ntsoane

"Who was it?" interjected Lekala.

"It was his son, Nko. It seemed he was trying to climb over the gate when it fell and trapped him," he said.

"Ouch! Was he hurt?" asked Lekala.

"He seemed to be in a lot of pain even though he was drunk. His call for help was languid," said Sekele.

"And then?" asked Lekala.

"I tried to lift the gate to free him but it was too heavy. It seemed whenever I tried to move it he was getting more hurt as he cried out viciously," he said.

"Oh, Lord!" exclaimed Lekala.

"There was no time to lose so I shouted for help, calling my neighbour Sakago to come and help me free the boy," Sekele said.

"Did he come out to help?" Lekala asked.

"No, he didn't," Sekele said.

"Oh, no!" all who were listening exclaimed at the same time. They were all ears, anxious to hear the rest of the story.

"You won't believe what happened thereafter," said Sekele.

"What happened?" asked Lekala anxious to hear the end of the tragic incident.

"Man, the lights of his house went out. I am sure he heard me because I saw his silhouette move towards the front window that was open. It was certainly him

©PJ Ntsoane

because I could not mistake his big tummy for anyone else's. He is the only one in the neighbourhood with that kind of an airbag in front of him. By the way his wife is not pregnant. She competes with her husband only when she is in that state. You know, you won't believe it. He closed the window and pulled the curtains before he switched off the lights," Sekele said shaking his head.

Other men who overheard the conversation of the two pulled their chairs closer to hear well. All of them were whistling and shaking their heads in bewilderment.

"Man, that is unbelievable," retorted Lekala.

"I could hardly believe it myself," replied Sekele.

"How can a true African man ignore another's cry for help?" asked Lekala.

"Realising that he was not coming to help me, I rushed to his door to knock. There was no time to lose. The boy was dying. You won't believe it, he also ignored my bangs on his door," said Sekele.

"Why would he do that? I mean even if he didn't hear your voice as it is so hoarse and faint from *mbamba* and *mablar* (illicit brew and dried tobacco leaves) that you are so addicted to, he would definitely have heard the bangs on the door," retorted Lekala.

The men who were listening chuckled when they heard Lekala give Sekele a taste of his own medicine. Sekele

©PJ Ntsoane

was the one who always enjoyed making fun of other people. He waggled his finger at Lekala and smiled.

"I shouted his name pleading with him to come out and help me as the boy was in danger. Still there was deafening silence," said Sekele.

"Neighbours are supposed to look out for each other. What kind of an African is this Sakago?" asked Lekala.

"I think he thought it was my son who was hurt because I was not mentioning the boy by his name. I think so because he only responded when I mentioned his son's name. He quickly switched on the lights and came out of the house huffing and puffing," said Sekele.

"So if it was your son he would not have come to your rescue?" asked Lekala.

"Definitely, I think he thought I had come to ask for transport to hospital since I don't have a car. His intention was to make me feel his power and importance," said Sekele.

"What a fool!" Lekala exclaimed.

All men who gathered to listen to the story concurred.

"That son of his is in hospital as we speak. He is in ICU. The gate has seemingly done the damage. I pray that he should get well soon. To think…" Sekele said when Lekala interrupted him.

"Did he thank you thereafter?" inquired Lekala. There was a pause as Sekele rolled up and licked his roll of

©PJ Ntsoane

tobacco. He was so meticulous with making a tobacco roll that his fellow smokers would always ask him to make one for them when they needed to be on fire.

"No, he didn't. Anyway I only thank God I came when I did, otherwise…" he said.

"How could an educated man like him behave like a savage?" asked Lekala.

"Sometimes the suits and ties we wear do not free us from our savagery," retorted Sekele.

"You could say that again," said Lekala.

"This world is full of amazing personalities," rejoined Sekele.

"This reminds me of a certain guy I grew up and went to school with called Joseph," added Lekala.

"What did he do?" asked Sekele.

"One rainy day I was walking home from work. I was walking along the road from the shopping mall. Man I had no umbrella with me as I had not expected rain on that particular day," said Lekala.

"I know what you looked like because I have experienced that several times," added Sekele.

"The guy is a clerk at one of the Government Departments and they have given him a subsidised car. You know we poor teachers do not have that luxury despite the many degrees we have. The guy hooted and passed by. I waved my hand in acknowledgement and

©PJ Ntsoane

continued walking. You know, he reappeared and this time going in the opposite direction. He hooted again as he drove passed. I waved my hand in acknowledgement and continued with my journey. Man, he reappeared for the third time going in the same direction. He hooted. This time I did not respond. I simply ignored him and continued walking. He slowed down and pulled over. He rolled down the glass of his front window and called out my name. I stopped and looked at him to hear what he wanted to say. I thought he was going to offer me a lift but I was wrong. He said, 'Hey mate, still a pedestrian? I would offer you a lift but you are too drenched as you can see. You will spoil my upholstery'. He squeaked away splashing me with muddy waters," said Lekala.

All those who were listening hollered in amazement. "What a spoiled elf!" Sekele retorted.

"That day I imagined how better this world would be if these cars on our roads were the ones with brains instead or if they symbolised their owners' intelligence," Lekala commented.

This same Joseph was a pastor at one of mushrooming churches in the country. He was famous as a motivational speaker and people found his sermons invigorating. He liked to preach about fraternity and peace. His trademark was, 'Thou shall love thy neighbour.' He also loved saying, 'Do unto others as you

©PJ Ntsoane

would have them do to you.' Lekala stopped attending his church because he could not tolerate that self-righteous hypocrite. He also heard from a reliable source that he had broken several marriages in the village despite acting as a self-appointed marriage counselor.

"I have heard that he divorced his wife of ages and married a young member of the church. It's said that when he divorced his wife he claimed that God had revealed to him in a vision that a suitable young woman in the congregation should become his wife. How pretentious!" exclaimed the seemingly irritated Sekele.

"If God had enabled us to see through others' hearts, these mischievous acts would not happen," said Lekala.

"Then we would have nothing to talk about. I think God did that for a reason" said Sekele.

©PJ Ntsoane

2

As they were chatting and savouring the stories, the court usher blew the *phalafala (*kudu horn) announcing the approach of the Chief and the royal elders. Praise singers bellowed praise-songs and all were on their feet. You don't sit down when the Chief approaches lest you are fined a cow. All are supposed to show loyalty by bowing and muttering: *'Sebata sa mabala, thoba dingwe melala'*-loosely translated it means: 'the ferocious one'. Thus, the Chief is compared to a leopard. The Chief ascended to his pedestal at a snail's pace. He would stop and turn around with a puckered brow. He bared his teeth and growled like an angry leopard before he sat down. All stood in attention waiting for an order to sit down. The Chief took his time examining his subjects with half closed drab eyes. There was a deafening silence. Nobody dared make a sound. Even those who had a cold held their urge to cough out phlegm. He then nodded his head as a sign that they could sit down. The court usher bellowed out, "You may all take your sits. The ferocious one welcomes you."

There was a buzz as the people were resuming their sits. A few seized the opportunity to execute a cough and a sneeze.

"Today we have a case brought by the Matobe family against their *makoti (*daughter-in-law), one Malesedi. It

©PJ Ntsoane

is common knowledge that her husband, the late Totoba, may his soul rest in peace, passed away tragically in mysterious circumstances two weeks ago," said Kakata, the court elder who is Chief Kgoratau's younger brother.

All agreed in a choral, '*Re tsebe ntlha, bolela sebata*' meaning: 'we are all ears, speak out the brave one'. The words were said in perfect orchestral timing. It seemed everybody knew when to say it and when to stop. People were taught to say that early in their lives.

"Before we hear their testimony, on behalf of the royal elders I would like to find out if the families are here with us. Please stand up and bow to the Ferocious One," said Kakata, who had a brazen voice that echoed in the mountains afar.

Kakata had a voice that was incompatible with his miniature stature. He was the wittiest in the whole village and of course with the exception of the Chief whose most imprudent decision would always be applauded. There was no case or problem that seemed to baffle Kakata. He had a penchant for black suits with white shirts and bright coloured ties. He was always immaculately dressed.

All Matobe elders were present but Malesedi's parents and elders had not yet arrived. However, their car could be seen down the valley. It was followed by a long trail

©PJ Ntsoane

of dust on the dirt road leading to Motsetona royal kraal. Malesedi stood up and tried to explain her people's unpunctuality. Kakata harshly ordered her to sit down as women were not expected to address the court standing up. She reluctantly complied with Kakata's orders. All men murmured that she was being disrespectful. You could see that they were prejudiced against her. She timidly stole a glance around the court yard that was already full of angry men and she felt a chill down her spine.

Her parents and elders ultimately arrived at the gates of the royal homesteads. Guards ushered them in by forming an uneasy guard of honour. They felt like prisoners without trial as they shuffled up towards the court yard. All eyes of those in the court seemed to pierce them like sharp spears. They were unbearable. They were shown their sits but before they were allowed to sit they had to greet the Chief and apologise for their late coming. "Your Excellency, please accept our apologies for keeping you waiting so long. It was not our intention to keep you waiting for us. It was beyond our control. Our car had a puncture when we joined the dirt road leading to this village. When we tried to replace it with a spare tyre unfortunately we found that it was flat as well. So we had to use a hand pump to inflate it. That is why it took us so long. We called our

©PJ Ntsoane

daughter Malesedi and asked her to convey the message to this court," said Raselepe, who was Malesedi's uncle.

Kakata recalled that he refused to allow Malesedi to address the Court earlier. Since he was not the one who was wont to apologise, he ignored Raselepe's entreaty.

"*Ga ba thibe marokgo a rena,*" the audience hollered meaning: 'they must mend our trousers'. In African tradition whoever is a respondent in a case has to pay dues to the court for attending to the matter.

"You will have to pay a goat to this court for making us wait so long for you. We are being lenient as you can see. We could have finished with your case but for your delay," said Kakata, expecting no comment from them.

"But your Excellency, with all due respect, this is too harsh on us. We didn't delay deliberately. Please bear with us," said Raselepe, showing signs of exasperation.

"It's finalised. There is nothing you can do to change it," concluded Kakata, seemingly annoyed.

Malesedi sat there anxious to say something. She raised her hand asking for an opportunity to express her opinion. Kakata reluctantly allowed her to have her say.

"Thank you your Excellency. I have only one question to ask this court. What would you do if while you were in the process of listening to a case, a thunder cloud burst

©PJ Ntsoane

onto this open court?" asked Malesedi who neither stood up nor raised her eyes to look at the audience.

There was murmuring as men scratched their heads in contemplation. Some nodded their heads in agreement while others shook theirs in amazement.

"The session would definitely be adjourned. What has that got to do with the fine?" asked Kakata.

"Your Excellency, the point I want to raise here is that there are certain circumstances that are beyond one's control. Those people did not puncture their car deliberately. You didn't even allow me to convey the message that they had asked me to. You don't even bother to verify their reasons by checking if indeed they have a flat tyre in the boot of their car. If you did that maybe you would find it in your heart to be a little lenient," said Malesedi, resting her case.

"You can't challenge our tradition woman. It's not a matter of veracity or leniency. The main point here is our cultural norm. If you make the court wait too long, you pay, period!" shouted Kakata.

Raselepe raised his hand and was allowed to talk.

"I abide by the law of our forefathers. What this young woman has just said shows all of you here that if you only keep bulls in your kraal you will not have milk. We need opinions of our women sometimes. They can make our blurred vision clear. I also obediently raise this

©PJ Ntsoane

point that this court has no jurisdiction over me. I have my own chief who is qualified to fine me. This fine you impose on me will instead be paid by your subjects. My daughter Malesedi's in-laws should bear the brunt. The goat that has to be paid should come from their kraal because we are here on account of them," said Raselepe.

"But they didn't arrive late, you did. Since you have committed the crime here at Motsetona, it stands to reason that you have to be charged and tried by this court," said Kakata.

"Oh, I am shivering now! Have we committed a crime? I didn't know that arriving late due to unforeseen and uncontrollable circumstances was a crime," said Raselepe.

"Oh, news-flash, it is a crime! Late coming is considered to be contempt of court. By the way, don't you know that people get dismissed for late coming?" asked Kakata.

"But still you have to charge me through my chief. It is disrespectful to charge the subject of another chief without his knowledge. In the past wars were fought over lesser issues," said Raselepe.

"Watch your tongue young man. Don't provoke us," said Kakata threateningly.

©PJ Ntsoane

Meanwhile the Chief cleared his throat, all immediately fell silent and a rendition of 'Sebata' reverberated in the court yard. He had been listening to the squabbling with half interest.

Kakata immediately announced that the court session would begin.

"All who are expected to attend are present. We can start in the name of our Chief, our ancestors and God the Creator of the universe. I shall call upon the plaintiff Matobe to give this Court his grievances. Matobe, the Court is all ears," Kakata said, retiring to his chair.

Lerumo, the interpreter, stood on his feet ready to report to the elders, who in turn repeated the same to the Chief as if he had not been listening. That was done so that the Chief would have enough time to analyse and think about the response he had to give.

Matobe stood up and bowed to the jury of elders and all in attendance. He cleared his throat in the example of those from royalty. He seemed full of confidence. He held onto his club tightly to prop himself up. It doubled up as a walking stick. The old man was suffering from arthritis, so standing up and walking without a stick was unthinkable.

"Your Excellency, this young woman was married to my eldest son Totoba, whom we buried two weeks ago as everyone knows. As you all know that according to our

©PJ Ntsoane

tradition a widow is expected to perform certain rites and wear all black to mourn her husband's passing, we were surprised when my daughter-in-law refused point blank that she would not do all those things. She refused in the presence of her parents and elders. Some tried to reason with her but she was adamant. We have brought her before this court so that you can help us with this matter as we regard it as disrespect of our culture. I know that His Excellency is the guardian of our tradition and will help us do justice," Matobe said and sat down.

Lerumo repeated the same to the elders who in turn conveyed the statement according to their rank until it 'reached the ears' of the Chief. The Chief merely nodded his head to show that he had heard what was said. The elders returned the answer according to their rank in descending order until it reached Lerumo. "Matobe, what reasons does your daughter-in-law give for her refusal to honour our traditional practices?" asked Kakata.

Matobe stood up again to answer. "She only said that it was against her belief. She says that she is not an uncivilised African who would observe customs that do not make sense. Your Excellency, if you allow me, she ridiculed our tradition. We felt so embarrassed and worthless after she had said all those things. I think she

©PJ Ntsoane

did not only insult us but the whole of Motsetona and neighbouring villages," said Matobe, this time not sitting down as if expecting a follow up question.

"What belief was she referring to?" asked Kakata.

"I can't really tell. She is the only one more qualified to explain," said Matobe.

"What do you want this Court to do?" asked Kakata.

"All I want is justice to be done," Matobe said.

All in the court yard murmured. Some were already agreeing with Matobe even before they heard Malesedi's own account. They were saying unprintable things about her. Others were even calling for her head. In their view no one, especially a woman, should be allowed to disrespect the ways of their ancestors.

"What justice are you talking about, Matobe?" asked Kakata.

"This young woman has dishonoured our being as a people. If I had my way, I would have her banished from this village. Her parents must return the entire bride's price we paid them when we married their good-for-nothing daughter," said Matobe.

There was a reverberation in the court yard as everybody was telling whoever cared to listen, what they were thinking about the matter.

"Order, stop your pocket meetings!" Kakata shouted.

©PJ Ntsoane

Everybody fell silent. No one dared defy Kakata's orders. He was wont to slapping members with heavy fines. He was so generous with fines that he was nicknamed 'Radifaini' meaning: 'Mr. Fines'. If he discovered that your kraal was getting full of sheep or goats he would slap you with a fine on slightest provocation. People who had livestock were always wary whenever they received a pretentious visit from his known spy Mankge. This man had a tendency to show up conveniently when herd-boys were returning with the livestock from the grazing fields. He would inspect the prospective victim's livestock and give hollow compliments whenever he spotted a fat sheep or goat that he would confiscate once an offence was expediently made for him. He was a nuisance one could not avoid or get rid of. If you evasively stayed away from court meetings when he had eyed your stock you would be given a fine for truancy. If you attended and treaded warily to avoid a fine he would slap you with a fine for a trivial reason like noise making. He was a real mosquito.

Now it was time for Malesedi to give her version of the story. She stood up. Kakata shouted that she should return to sitting position in compliance with the culture of the people. She protested and before she sat down she told the court that she would not utter a word until

©PJ Ntsoane

she was allowed to speak standing up like everybody else. Malesedi sat down and kept quiet. All attempts to make her talk were in vain as she sat there with her eyes fixed on the ground. There was a stalemate that could only be broken by the Chief himself. He cleared his throat and everybody suddenly kept quiet.

"I have heard and seen all that transpired here today. I postpone the trial to the morning of next Friday to give Balepe time to talk with their daughter and they must not come here to waste our time again. All dismissed," Chief Kgoratau said.

All shouted their Chief's praises in unison. They were quickly on their feet like well drilled soldiers. They waited for the Chief to disappear into his royal house before they could disperse.

©PJ Ntsoane

3

Malesedi was disturbed by what happened at the Royal Court. She told herself that she needed to put her education to good use by liberating men and women in the villages. She resolved to help break the shackles of archaic practices. There were many who were suited and tied in the name of tradition. She remembered her grandfather's words as he used to say: 'If those who have the light do not switch it on, the ones in darkness will never see the beauty of the scenery.'

She moved around the village during the day when the men were at work, selling the idea of a women's organisation to housewives. She invited them to a meeting scheduled for Monday of the following week. She asked the women not to mention a thing to their husbands for fear of sabotage. The meeting was scheduled for 12 o'clock in the afternoon when all housewives would have completed their morning chores. The attendance was not as expected because only ten women turned up. Malesedi told herself that she had to do her best by inspiring those present so that they became advocates of women's course.

They opened the meeting with a prayer and Malesedi stood up to address them. She was a tall woman who

©PJ Ntsoane

could have easily become a super-model if she wanted. Many men felt dwarfed in her presence.

"My sisters, I greet you in the name of our Creator. I am glad that you heeded my invitation to come to this gathering. As you can see, our agenda is very limited. I hope next time the number of women attending will be bigger and the agenda longer. That is if you go out there and spread the revolutionary message to our sisters and brothers who need liberation. I know that you are wondering what I am talking about," she paused to look at their reaction. All the women looked at each other in amazement. Indeed they were lost.

"Sisters, as you can see I am talking to you standing up. Would I be allowed to do the same if this meeting included men? I don't think so. Our menfolk are blinded by their misguided patriarchy. They treat us as if we are nonentities only when it suits them. Those of us who were lucky to be wooed would recall how pathetic these men looked when they wanted our acceptance. We could sense fear in their tones when they begged us to accept their sorry pleas. Some of them even boasted to their friends thereafter that they were charmers. But we know reality because we could see desperation in their sorry eyes. These men worshipped the ground we walked on. But the moment we relented and they got what they wanted they treated us like used toilet paper.

©PJ Ntsoane

How long are we going to allow these men to treat us like dirt? I don't think there is any woman who is worth her salt who can allow a self-serving patriarch to run rough-shot on her back. We need to reclaim our rightful place and status. That is by the side of our men-folk, not behind them. We need equal treatment. Is there any man who can bear a child? Yet they claim our children as theirs when they do well. It makes them feel powerful. When a child is not performing very well they shift the blame to us.

They don't know the pain of child labour, but whenever our daughters are getting married they are the ones who negotiate the *magadi* (dowry). We, the mothers can only make do with what is reported to us. And what is funny is that after reaching their agreement they expect us to ululate for them as their hoarse voices will even scare off cats and dogs. We can't allow this to continue. Don't ever think that these people will give you concessions willingly. We need to knock sense into their thick skulls without delay," Malesedi said, pausing to feel the audience's reaction.

"But our husbands are providing for our families. How shall we survive without their support?" asked Makutumela, her face showing signs of fear.

"Yes, they provide for us. That is a good thing if they do that honestly. But are we consulted whenever the

©PJ Ntsoane

family budget is made? The answer is a capital NO? They think we are not intelligent enough to make good decisions. That is the reason for their condescending. And we abet our own oppression if we accede to that," Malesedi retorted.

"Is it not against tradition to challenge the authority of our husbands? Is it not written in the Book you read in Church that the man is the head of the family as well?" asked Mamaila.

"It is called the Bible, Mamaila. My husband always reads to us that God created a man in his own image first. That man was Adam," said Mapule.

Malesedi looked anxious. She realised how brainwashed some of the women were. How was she going to convince them otherwise? She suspected that these weakest links would reveal to their husbands what Malesedi was planning to do and thus scupper her plans. It is not easy to convince non-believers. However, it was an arduous task that she had to perform. Indeed, she had to serve her mission on earth. She felt a sting in her heart and started sweating in the palm of her hands. She quickly opened her handbag and took out a white handkerchief to wipe her sweaty forehead and fan up.

"Yes God created man in His own image. You must know that man refers to mankind. The woman who was created for Adam was meant to be his helpmate with

©PJ Ntsoane

rights. Okay, are we treated as helpers with rights? No, we are worse than slaves. In fact men are traitors because God never made a slave for Adam but a companion with equal rights," Malesedi replied.

The women looked at each other and timidly nodded. They were beginning to see the light.

"Sisters, we must break the stranglehold that these men have on us as sole breadwinners. It is emotional blackmail. We need to be able to make our own money so that we become independent," she said.

"We are not educated. How are we going to do that," asked Mamaila.

"There are many ways to generate income. We can form cooperatives or a *stokvel* (a club for the pulling of mutual fund*s)* to help ourselves. This is done by women all over the continent and they have recorded successes. If they could do it, so can we. We also need to introduce adult education classes. Many women in this area are disadvantaged because they are illiterate. Illiteracy makes you a prisoner of circumstances. You tend to fear the unknown and have no guts to face challenges. You begin to regard your husband as a refuge. You can't see yourself surviving without him. We can free ourselves, sisters. Don't ever think that our oppressors have our interest at heart. Do you hope that one day they are going to wake up and hand over our

©PJ Ntsoane

freedom on a platter? All you need is ambition and passion for the course of liberation," said Malesedi.

The women became restless as it was getting late. Their husbands and sons would be returning from work and grazing fields so they had to go home to prepare hot meals for them. It was an offence for a woman not to give her husband a hot dish upon arrival. Many women in the village were severely whipped and sent back to their parents for the same offence. Malesedi noticed the women's uneasiness and decided to release them. She didn't want to alienate them so early. They were foot soldiers that needed strategic training. She had to win their trust.

"Sisters I know that you have to go and prepare meals for your families. That is good. You know, we are the axles of our families. I only wish our counterparts could appreciate that and stop turning us into punching bags whenever it suits them. We shall meet again in two days' time. Please spread the revolutionary word and recruit soldiers," Malesedi said in conclusion.

The women burst into a defiant women's song- *Basadi, basadi kopanang* which means: 'women unite'.

As they were about to disperse they heard someone sneeze in the tree under which they had been meeting. They almost froze with fright when they realised that

©PJ Ntsoane

the royal spy, Sepekwa was up in the tree. He had probably heard every word they said and was going to report to the Chief. He was a renowned snoop dog who sniffed out all 'enemies' of the royal house. He was nicknamed 'The eagle eyes' because he could see the minutest of activities in the village. Some even suspected him of having eyes and ears that could penetrate the walls of all houses in the village and afar. Now the women demanded that he climb down so they could deal with him once and for all. Sepekwa refused to budge because he could sense fire in the women's voices so he would not risk being in the path of angry dragons. He tried to reason with them.

"Ladies, I have done nothing wrong. When you came here I was already up in the tree. I only came here because I was looking for my lost sheep. I climbed the tree so I could view the surrounding area instead of going from one end to another. I have no business eavesdropping. Besides I truly support women emancipation, *Amandla* (Power)!" Sepekwa shouted.

They made a lot of hullaballoo as all tried to speak at the same time. They were wagging their fingers at Sepekwa up in the tree, calling him names.

"Sepekwa, do you want to feel women's fury?" Malesedi asked.

©PJ Ntsoane

"What wrong have I done now? I didn't ask or force you to come to this tree. You came here of your own free will. In fact you are the ones who intruded. You came here and disturbed my peace," said Sepekwa.

"We didn't know that you were up there" Mamaila said.

"Rubbish, how can you miss the smell of my perfume? You women have a good sense of smell," Sepekwa quipped.

"I smelt tobacco whiff but thought it was transported by wind from afar. Anyway how would we know it was distinctly yours?" asked Malesedi.

"You never know who can distinguish that on a darkest night. You women pretend that you don't like us but you would kill to have us warm your beds," Sepekwa retorted.

"Don't insult us. Who would have a brewery like you for a lover?" Malesedi said.

"Please don't provoke me. I can shame all of you if I want to. You forget that I can see anything that happens secretly in this village even in the cover of the night or inside your rooms," said Sepekwa.

"You overrate yourself. If you go and blab a word of what transpired here today you will wish you were never born. We will make you vanish into thin air. That is a promise," Malesedi threatened.

"Are you talking from experience?" asked Sepekwa.

©PJ Ntsoane

"No, you will be our first experience. The only regret is you will not be there to bear testimony," Malesedi said.

When the women realised that Sepekwa was not going to come down they quickly dispersed and disappeared into the dusk horizon. Sepekwa watched their silhouette figures disappearing up the slope and wondered if they meant what they said. He felt intimidated by women for once in his life time. He would feel embarrassed if any of those women told her husband about their encounter. Men would make a mockery of him all the time.

©PJ Ntsoane

4

The Chief ordered Kakata to call an emergency meeting of the inner circle of the royal elders. He seemed disturbed when he issued the order. Kakata was wondering what could have disturbed His Majesty but complied because no one dared question the Chief. If asked a question, he would give the poser a stern gaze and bite his lower lip you would think blood would ooze out. He would speak whenever he felt he was ready or willing.

The Council gathered as soon as possible. There was someone who was conspicuous by his absence, Sepekwa. He never missed a Council meeting even when he was down with severe flu. He would drag himself out of bed and saunter to the Court. Whenever members asked him why he didn't stay at home since he was sick he would say: 'I am not going to let chicken disease hold me down. I am a lion. I only need a nip of *Makhura'Sepekwa* (African home-brewed gin) then I will be fine.' He made the drink so popular in the village that many men gave it the name associated with him. The brew is so high in alcohol that only a tot would knock the strongest man down. When a person has gulped a few tots you would see by the way he walked. The drunk would take two steps forward and one step backward. There were few women in the village who

©PJ Ntsoane

were adept at production of the drink. It needed outstanding skill and patience if ever you wanted to be proficient. The brew was illicit and those who produced it were often arrested by the local police. Despite harassment by the police the brewers never gave up. They contended that the police were promoting white businesses since they also produced dry gins similar to theirs. The only difference was that their counterparts had the right to sell them to the public. They wondered why some retail stores were allowed the sale of an assortment of the hot stuff copied from them but denied the originators that opportunity as small traders. They even claimed that the ones produced by white breweries were very expensive and their people could hardly afford them.

Chief Kgoratau cleared his throat and all members fell silent.

"My brothers, I have called this emergency meeting because of some crucial incidents that have occurred and require us to bring our heads together as leaders of the people," he said.

"We are all ears, Your Majesty," they all said in chorus.

"The first one concerns Sepekwa. He is fighting for his life in hospital after he was attacked by unknown assailants last night. He was left for dead. Had he not been found by a passerby he could have become an

©PJ Ntsoane

ancestor by now," Kgoratau said with tremor in his voice.

It became apparent why Sepekwa was unusually absent. Those gathered were horrified by the sad news.

"Another burning issue involves the visit by Inspector Masisi of the local police station. He brought a written memorandum from the Minister of Health which indicates a concern about a growing number of people from this area who are suffering from lung and liver diseases. They claim that the culprits in the whole matter are brewers of 'illicit' drinks patronised by the sufferers. They threaten to conduct a surprise raid of the villages if we do not curb this scourge. Now I want you to look into this matter as community elders," Kgoratau said.

"We hear you, The Brave One. By the way, who does Sepekwa say his attackers were?" asked Mankge.

"He can't say as he is unable to talk. If he knew how to write he would have helped with investigations as the police have taken up the matter. We need to take a word out to everyone so that whoever has information can come forward so that those responsible will be brought to book," said Kgoratau.

"These kinds of incidents are uncommon in our village. We must have lost our touch as keepers of order.

©PJ Ntsoane

Indeed, we need to nip the cancer of crime in the bud before it eats away at our social fibre," said Mankge.

"Of course we don't want to be the butt of our enemies. We need to make the wayward toe the line. But I am only disturbed by this matter concerning the planned banning of the brew that has been with us since time immemorial. The secret method and recipe was handed down to us by our ancestors. Don't these white people always talk about intellectual property rights? Besides, those mothers who produce the drink make our people happy. Some of them have even managed to keep the wolf from the door and put children through colleges or university with the income they make from their business. Guess what? The agents of colonial authorities are saying ours is not real business but the so-called informal sector. They have taken away everything from us: the land, languages, culture, and even our women. Women have become rebellious because they are taught that they have equal rights with us. Enough is enough. We must resist this insult and provocation," Mopedi added.

"I couldn't agree with you more. This morning my wife told me that she was tired and could not cook for me. She even suggested that I cook for myself and wash the dishes. Can you believe it? I was so irate that I nearly hit her with my club. What has this world come to? If we

©PJ Ntsoane

don't stand up and show these women who claim to be educated that God made us men for a reason, our ancestors will turn against us," Maita said.

"That is right! You have hit the mark, Maita. Our ancestors are probably turning in their graves because of all these shenanigans," Kutumela added.

"Brothers, I must call a mass meeting of all the adults of this village. We need to stamp authority and deal with those who want to make our ways a mockery," said Kgoratau.

"It is long overdue your Majesty. Our culture is virtually wiped by foreign elements. If we don't stand up now as real men and guardians of our forefathers' ways we will soon be extinct. I was also taken aback last night when I returned from the forest when I found my wife not home and the pots were not yet ready. I nearly strangled her because she couldn't give me any credible reason. She only said that she had been attending a women's club meeting. Can you believe it? She had the audacity to say that she was tired and ordered my daughter to cook for us. I felt like the world had turned upside down. I didn't touch the damn food. I went to my other wife's hut. Fortunately she had dished out. Just imagine if I had only one wife, I would definitely have gone to bed on an empty stomach," said Rapula.

©PJ Ntsoane

"There must be something that these women are planning at these meetings of theirs. How could they display the same behaviour at the same time? We need to find out what they talk about at these meetings. We need to be a step ahead of them. If we are not careful, we shall kiss our manhood goodbye," said Maita.

"I hear you, brothers. We must infiltrate this emerging subversive organisation. Every fortress has a weak spot. We can't be outwitted by our women. The fact that we courted and charmed them into marrying us shows who the powerful are," said Kakata.

"Hey you must be careful there. Some of these women were coerced into marrying us. There are some of us who were so timid that the women they married only felt sorry for them. That is why they are at the mercy of their wives. They can't control their women at all. These are the ones who must be corrected too. They are letting the manhood down," said Kutumela.

"Yeah, their weakness is a letdown. It will be cancerous if we do not deal with it effectively. I have someone I think will help give us inside information," said Kakata.

"Who is that?" asked Kutumela.

"I think it would be better if I kept her name a secret lest one of you brothers blabs unconsciously when in the comfort of the bed of one of the insurgents," said Kakata.

©PJ Ntsoane

The men looked at each other sheepishly and laughed. For a moment they realised the power that the women had. They silently reminisced about their moments of bliss with the fairer counterparts and acknowledged their vulnerability. If ever they were to win the war they had to work against that weak point in their system. Women are known to be secretive in African culture. They would go with a secret to their graves if needs be. Their moment of weakness would only be when they are engaged in a confrontation with other women. It would be the only time you hear about their opponent's bones in the closet.

©PJ Ntsoane

5.

The day of the mass meeting arrived. All adults under Chief Kgoratau from all corners of the country came. The royal court yard was abuzz with song, ululations and laughter. Everything seemed to be in order. Those with the means were dressed to kill. Men dressed in their best tuxedos which they had taken to the dry-cleaners for the occasion and women in dresses that would make the onlookers eat their hearts out.

"Silence!" shouted Kakata, "today we have an unusual gathering. Rules have been relaxed. That is why we are not going to be graced with The Brave One's presence. This is the meeting of the subjects only. The Chief wants us to make our inputs since He leads by our will. This is our land, our tribe and our destiny. Fellow residents our land has been invaded. There are foreign elements that are disturbing the purity, peace and quiet of our area. The onus is upon us to defend our integrity, the essence of our being. I am going to hand over to Lerumo to describe to us the beasts that have invaded our kraal."

Lerumo stood up. He had a spear in his hand. It was a token of bravery that symbolised his lineage of warriors. He was the tallest man in the area. He had stout broad shoulders, long strong gorilla arms and blood shot eyes that seemed to pierce the heart of whoever looked into them. He cleared his throat, "Greetings followers of The

©PJ Ntsoane

Great One." He waited for a thunderous response from all and sundry.

"We are here today to either save or further sink this great tribe. There are criminals who run rough shot over this area. They attack villagers and steal their hard earned belongings. These people are members of our households. There are people among us who harbour these unwanted elements. Remember the weeds of destruction can only prosper if those who have hoes do not uproot them.

One other thing is the police who have criminalised home brewing of our traditional beer. Lastly some women and children are disrespecting our ways which I am afraid is going to make us the laughing stock of other nations. Now we would like to hear what you have to say about it," he concluded and sat down.

Peu, a man who was renowned for his frankness stood up to talk. He cleared his throat and cast his gaze around the full court yard.

"Basically the main source of all the problems is the system that has turned our own people as clandestine agents of oppression. We are dispossessed and our oppressors have only replaced their faces with those of our own. These individuals who unfortunately look like our brothers and sisters are subtly selfish and arrogant. They line their own pockets and fill their bellies with

©PJ Ntsoane

'good boy' incentives from our exploiters. They speak our language and claim to be the voice of the voiceless. We are not voiceless. Let us not allow our oppressors to patronise us. Let us show them that we have seen through their lies as they are as transparent as clear water in a river. Now, for instance, we have lost our best farm land to a few foreign controlled cooperatives masquerading as community empowerment projects. Our people are swindled into believing that they are engaged in participatory development when they are actually modern slaves. The proceeds from their products disappear into the so-called operational costs and capital building. The few executives are the ones who cash in on these schemes as they get hefty pay cheques and bonuses. They do not shed a drop of sweat but justify the expensive cars they drive on promotional image or security rhetoric. Those of us who do the spade work often go home empty handed. Our children are dismissed from school because we cannot keep up with exorbitant fees. We aren't even entitled to a few of our products as they are exported to foreign lands. Do you know how torturing it is to look at those tantalising oranges, apples, grapes, and avocadoes when you are hungry? You look at them and think that you produced these but you cannot afford to buy them for your own children. There were many of the workers who were

©PJ Ntsoane

dismissed for eating some of those fruits. They would rather see you faint from hunger than allow you to eat one of machine rejected fruits. Our people dig up those minerals that turn only a few into billionaires. These mines that we have in this area have taken our livestock's grazing fields. Our cattle are impounded when they are found on the roads or near the mine bosses' residential areas. The part of the river that God had given us is now fenced off as private property. Our livestock does not have drinking water. We have to travel many kilometres to water them at the almost dry communal part of the river which is denied water supply because the companies and foreign owners have diverted the water into their huge dams.

One of our brothers, Lesiba lost all his cattle because they were auctioned out and sold for a song. This was because he had no idea that they had been taken by the police who found them grazing on the road near the mine owners' residences as our small grazing field was exhausted. His whole heritage is now gone. To rub salt into the wound, one of his cousins told him that one of his bulls was slaughtered by the mine bosses at their end of the year party. That cousin of his was never offered a piece of steak for a *braai* (barbecue) even when he had helped in the whole preparations. He said he nearly cried when he recognised the bull before it

©PJ Ntsoane

was slaughtered. How is Lesiba going to feed his family when he does not even have educational qualifications for employment? Besides, even if he had any they would reject him on account of his age. To add to the woes, employment in many of the state-owned companies is influenced by bureaucracy. Only the crones and family members of the executives get opportunities. The real heirs of this land are passed by. This is pathetic to say the least," Peu said, wiping beads of sweat from his face.

The audience roared in agreement. The debate flared up into a variety of complaints. It was disclosed that many of the families had left the graves of their ancestors on the farms which were taken over by expatriates, local white farmers and mining companies from the East. They said that they could not visit those graves to clean them or to perform their traditional rituals. Those who dared venture to those places were arrested for trespassing. One family was denied the right to fulfill the last wish of their mother who had passed away. She had asked her children to bury her next to her late husband who died young and was buried in the place that was bought by a foreign national from a local farmer, who was only happy to cash in on wealthy property investors' desire to have land in as many different countries as possible. To make

©PJ Ntsoane

matters worse the foreign wealthy property owner kept game on the farm. The fertile land where the natives used to produce massive harvest had wild animals roaming around. The new owner enjoyed bringing his rich friends over to hunt and shoot game for fun. It was rumoured that they often held hunting competitions which had huge prizes to be won. It was common knowledge that some of the traditional chiefs and local councilors reached an agreement with those rich people in exchange for ludicrous gifts. It was said that they were invited to meetings in town and booked into five star hotels where they were served delicacies by tantalising hostesses before they were duped into signing their lands away. Some of them didn't understand the contents of the contracts. They took the word of negotiators who declared their good intentions about the development and beneficiation for the local residents. They painted their projects with such glowing colours that the leaders were blown away. One chief was given a car as a gift. Others had mansions built for them. That convinced them into believing in the good intention of the prospectors. The chiefs were suited and tied so they would become easy prey to economic predators. Some altruistic local elites who tried to intervene were brushed aside like chuff. They were accused of being anti-progress and opportunistic. Smear

©PJ Ntsoane

campaigns were launched against them. There were some who were unfortunate as they died or disappeared mysteriously. Investigations into the cause of deaths always faded into thin air as they were inconclusive. Malesedi's husband was one of the regional leaders who had formed a concerned group whose main objective was to fight against disinheritance of their people.

Lesiba felt that it was opportune time for him to add to what his fellow villagers were saying. He could not keep mum when his plight had been bared to the whole village.

"Yes, it is true that these old and new systems have disempowered us. Our chiefs do as they wish because they believe that our communal land belongs to them alone. Political leaders on the other hand also believe that they are more entitled to the God given resources in our area. To my surprise this new system is called democracy which means the government according to the will of the people. What we see around here is a farce. Yes we vote every seven years but our wishes are ignored. We cannot make a living from the land left for us. It is not enough. Our children do not get employment in the cities. One of my sons lives in a shack in an informal settlement near the big city. He says they do not have anything decent despite the fancy

©PJ Ntsoane

name given to the place. There is no sanitation, water and electricity. He says it looks like a pig-sty when it rains. They are harassed by criminals and there is nothing they can do about it as the police there say they should not take the law into their own hands. They are despondent. I have asked him to come back home but he refused as there is nothing to come back to. It is like jumping out of a frying pan and falling into the fire. Now when our women are trying to make a living through their home brew, they are declared criminals. What are we supposed to do brothers and sisters?" asked Lesiba.

Women who were unconventionally in attendance kept quiet and listened to the men expressing their dominant opinions. It seemed like they had succumbed to patriarchy until Mabotse raised her hand requesting an opportunity to declare her opinion. She knelt down as women were not allowed to speak standing up.

"Thank you for this opportunity my elders. As a young mother I am concerned about the livelihood of my children. You see I represent women who depend on their husbands for provision of household necessaries. Before I got married at a young age I had dreams of becoming a career woman. I was doing well at school even though the distance on foot was killing us. I was determined to pass so that I could be someone young girls would look up to. To my dismay, poverty at home

©PJ Ntsoane

occasioned by the loss of our fields to the mining company popped the bubble of my fantasy. I was forced into a marriage that my parents arranged because they convinced me that it was for the best. I was naïve then but now I know the mistake that it was. I have heard some of you defend women who brew alcohol in this area. My lords, I beg to differ. I am personally the victim of what you are defending. My husband was a very caring man after we got married. He changed into someone I have no words to describe after developing the habit of patronising those taverns you want to promote. Whenever he comes home drunk my children and I have palpitations as we are subjected to untold abuse. It kills me whenever I see my children huddled in the corner of the room with their starry eyes, shivering because they are afraid of their father who has turned into a monster. I came to this court several times and you my elders have not helped me as you claim that a man has authority and the right to do as he pleases. We don't want income at the expense of family happiness and moral fibre. We want decent jobs that will help us raise our children in a responsible way so that they become good citizens of this country. I think that you should be talking about the creation of cooperatives and clubs that will create sustainable income for all of us. I mean we need to be competitive in a responsible

©PJ Ntsoane

manner. Let us learn from other nations what they do to survive. It is possible for us to beat poverty in a just manner. Let us use the scarce resources we have to the maximum. If we work together as a community we can be exemplary to other nations as well. Yes, we have been dispossessed but that does not mean we should destroy the little we have. Charity begins at home. If families are well organised we are going to build a prosperous community that other villages are going to look up to. What I have observed my elders is that, if you may excuse me, we are obsessed with gender politics. Many of the fathers in this community harbour this empty pride of saying they do not listen to women. This is despite the fact that these women have a good point. We cannot even talk to our boys after their return from initiation school in the mountains. They become rebellious. It is heart breaking, my elders. Let us unite to fight the common cause as equals. I stop here and thank you again," Mabotse said, returning to her sedentary position.

There was a suppressed murmur as men and women expressed their mixed feelings about Mabotse's input. Maita stood up to speak, "Fellow men, I have heard what Mabotse said. She has a good point when it comes to family issues. We all know that a big village like ours is made up of households. Villages form a tribe and

©PJ Ntsoane

tribes constitute a nation. So a family is regarded as the foundation of every nation. We all know very well that a house built on a sandy foundation will not stand. Our elders taught us that a rowdy house shall not stand or produce a leader. The only way we can revitalise our cultural family values is if women understand that men are the heads of their families. I have a problem with Mabotse's suggestion that we should suddenly become equals. We shall never be equals. God didn't create us as equals. Our people have a saying that, '*Batho ga re lekane re se meno*' – loosely translated it means there has to be leaders and subordinates. We can work together, which is very crucial, but we all must know our positions. Women must know where they stand," he said.

Before Maita could sit down a commotion of people singing and approaching the court yard was heard. It was a group of women chanting songs of defiance. As the group entered the yard they could see that it was Malesedi and her friends. They were all wearing pairs of trousers usually worn by men. Kakata and Lerumo rushed forward to try and stop them before they mingled with the crowd. The women ran around the yard singing their songs in defiance.

Kakata called on several royal security guards to assist in removing the embarrassing nuisance from the court

©PJ Ntsoane

yard. The men took out their belts to try to intimidate the protestors. Their effort acted like fuel on fire as other women joined in the song and dance. The men could not believe their eyes when their wives dared them defiantly. All they could do was to issue futile threats to deal with their wives respectively when they arrived at home. The problem was how they would threaten those who did not have husbands. There was such commotion that the Chief was forced to call the police to come and quell the fire of anger in his own court yard. The women carried placards which showed that they were tired of being treated as second class or nonentities by the menfolk. Malesedi, like an army commander, directed the women to stop singing for a while and take orders for the next action. There was an abrupt deafening silence as the women stood in attention. She told Kakata and Lerumo to call the chief so that they could present their grievances. The men could not believe what these women were demanding. No one told the chief what to do because if you did you could be saddled with a huge fine or even banished from the area.

"Women, how dare you demand that the Chief should come to you? Do you know how serious that is?" asked Kakata.

©PJ Ntsoane

"Yes we know how serious it is. That is why we are protesting. If you do not comply we are going to disrupt this meeting and stage a sit in here forever," Malesedi said emphatically.

"Okay, the Chief is not well today. Let me take the message. I will deliver it to him accordingly," said Kakata.

"Our demands are summed up in this manner: *equal rights and justice for women*. To clarify it let me say, what you do for the boy child do it for the girl child as well. If a boy child has the right to speak standing up at a royal meeting so should the girl child. If a boy child has the right to step into the shoes of his father when he dies, so must the girl child. Now for instance the head wife in this royal kraal has only girls. She forfeits to directly provide this tribe with the next chief when the current one passes on. Is that fair? What sin have we committed as women to be disadvantaged in this manner? The first born of this royal house is very educated as a lawyer who studied Indigenous Law among others. She passed her grades just like her male counterparts. She even outclassed some of her male course mates. I was there when she graduated. She was the only one who obtained her degree *cum laude*. Do you see how ironic that is?" asked Malesedi.

©PJ Ntsoane

"Who are you to challenge the ways of our ancestors? I don't even know why I am holding this conversation with you. I cannot talk with a woman who is wearing trousers to make a mockery of our culture. You are going to be severely punished for this insubordination you, young woman," said Kakata turning away from the women.

As he turned there appeared in the valley a cloud of dust as the police vans made their way towards the royal court with their sirens wailing. In a moment they screeched to a stop in the court yard. Kakata commented that the unruly would feel the might of the law. The police in their uniforms scampered out of the vans carrying guns and wearing riot balaclava. Kakata raised his hand towards them drawing their attention. Surprisingly all the members of the police unit were women. Their captain went to Kakata and they shook hands. They exchanged a few words and walked towards the crowd in the royal kraal.

"People, listen carefully. We are now graced with the presence of law enforcers. They are here on the invite of the Chief. So I am going to call upon you troublemakers to vacate the royal kraal or else you will be arrested. These police are here to bring peace and safety," said Kakata.

©PJ Ntsoane

Malesedi moved forward. She appeared more agitated and toughened up. "Look who is talking? The very police you seem to be proud of are women. They are wearing uniform trousers. You do not find a problem with that. You only have a problem if trousers are worn by women in this village. They talk to you standing up and still you do not have a problem with it. We have seen you shake hands with the woman captain who is wearing trousers. Can you now see that forbidding us from performing certain acts on the basis that we are women is baseless?" Malesedi asked.

Kakata looked at Malesedi with a frown and shook his head. He turned to the police captain and nodded at her. She moved forward to speak to the women. Everybody listened attentively to hear what she had to say. Many expected her to sympathise with the women's course as she was a female herself.

"Listen here you all. We are here to keep law and order. There will be no problem as long as you follow my orders. Remember we will use the full might of the law if needs be. All you who are here uninvited must leave immediately. I give you five minutes to do that. If you don't I am afraid I will use force. Are we clear? Your time starts now," the Captain said.

Malesedi and the other women could not believe what they heard. They hurled insults at the police calling

©PJ Ntsoane

them traitors. Tension in the atmosphere could be cut with a knife.

"For your information Captain, we were all invited here as members of this community. They never mentioned us as excluded from the meeting. Unless the Chief shows us evidence that there are people who were barred from this meeting even when they are members of this community we will not move an inch," Malesedi said sitting down to show her determination. All the women in the yard did the same. The Captain ordered the officers to get ready for action. When the five minutes time elapsed the police advanced and tried to disperse the crowd. There was pandemonium as teargas canisters were flying amid baton wielding police who arrested Malesedi and other ring leaders. People in this village had never experienced an incidence of this nature. They were choked by the teargas and their eyes were severely stung by the chemical. Everybody ran helter-skelter and dispersed to safety while the troublemakers were whisked away in police vans.

©PJ Ntsoane

<u>6</u>

The Chief woke up the next morning with swollen eyes and sore throat. He could barely see or utter a word. He blamed it on witchcraft. He quickly summoned the head traditional doctor to come and exorcise the curse.

It is a traditional norm that a chief should have a contingent of strong traditional doctors to ward off or foretell imminent curses. The head doctor arrived with his paraphernalia of bones, claws, and indescribable teeth. The Chief summoned him into his hut. The hut was the one used by his father, the late chief. The only thing that changed about the old hut was the grass roof that was replaced several times whenever it was worn out. It was in that hut where he felt close to his ancestors. The traditional doctor scattered his bones to make his diagnosis.

"My Chief, I see a dark cloud hanging over you. This cloud has the face of a woman. The wind driving this cloud is blowing away your leopard skin and your hat. I see the wind removing these symbols of chieftaincy and placing them on the head and shoulders of a woman. There is much celebration around this cloud as small clouds also in the shape of women and girls move around excitedly. I can't really make out who they are," Mafahlela, said.

©PJ Ntsoane

"It must be that witch Malesedi and her friends. They are the ones who have been stirring trouble in this area lately. They must be the ones who are trying to bewitch me. I must deal with them once and for all. They are abusing my kindness in the name of democracy. She will vanish just like her husband. I only feel sorry for her parents. Since she came to this village there is no peace. Look at what happened to Sepekwa, I suspect that she is responsible for his attack. If only he could speak so that he tells us who attacked him. If they do not go to jail for a very long time you must do something about it as the head traditional doctor. I do not pay you to let people dance on my head," said the Chief.

"There is a strong force behind these people. It is going to be difficult for me to weaken them but it is not impossible. I'll do my best,"Mafahlela promised.

"I want you to ask your bones to tell us who exactly are responsible for Sepekwa's attack," Chief Kgoratau said.

Mafahlela muttered something like he didn't know if they would be able to identify the culprits. He picked up his bones and put them in their pouch. He asked the Chief to blow into the pouch three times as he entreated the bones to reveal who was responsible for the incident. The bones displayed the same information again. Chief Kgoratau was so amazed and infuriated at the same time. He could slightly read the fall of the

©PJ Ntsoane

bones himself. He was sure that the bones were right that he called the investigating detective to inform him about the breaking of the mystery behind Sepekwa's case. He was surprised to learn that the evidence he had would not stand in a court of law.

"Your bones won't be able to testify against whoever is suspected. They are not like a DNA test. The judge will even charge us for wasting his time with nonsense. I don't want to be made a laughing stock in the court. Anyway, we are closing in on the culprits. We will definitely make an arrest soon. I ask you not to take the law into your own hands because we will arrest you if you accuse or harm anyone," said the Police Sergeant.

The Chief dropped the phone on the police sergeant without saying goodbye. He called him names thereafter accusing him of laziness and corruption.

"These useless scumbags!" exclaimed Kgoratau, "they get fat salaries for doing nothing. I give him information that would help put this woman away for a very long time and he throws it back at me. They are suited and tied to foreign culture. They claim to be civilised by not believing in African ways. The bones can't lie. They waste time trying to find the truth from wrong doers who are conveniently called suspects. How can they implicate themselves, huh? They sit there in prison being treated like kings and queens even though they

©PJ Ntsoane

are guilty, nonsense!" he fumed. The traditional doctor was showing signs of nervousness as he grimaced whenever the Chief cursed. He realised how serious the issue was.

"What do you want me to do with these women who are trying to topple you. I can cast a spell and turn them into mutes. They will only use their hands to communicate when I am done with them. Just say the word all will be fixed," said Mafahlela.

Chief Kgoratau looked into the distance and mused for a while. He asked himself many questions concerning his own interests, chieftaincy, subjects and progeny. He had to do what was best for his legacy and the future of the community. He didn't want history to judge him harshly as the one who destroyed the pillars of tradition.

"I want to teach those responsible a lesson they will never forget. I want it to be a deterrent to those who would dare challenge my authority. I want you to strike them dumb. They must not be able to utter a word thereafter. They must only be able to communicate through sign language," said Kgoratau.

"Your wish is my command, my Lord. Please don't regret this because once it is done it won't be reversed," warned Mafahlela.

©PJ Ntsoane

"How can I regret punishing those who want to hurt me? They deserve the full wrath of the ancestors. They will be reaping what they have sown," said Kgoratau.

Mafahlela picked up his stuff and left without uttering another word. Chief Kgoratau new that once his order was issued it was like a launched missile. It either hit the target or got destroyed by anti-missile warhead.

Kakata budged into the hut where Chief Kgoratau was sitting. He was huffing and puffing. His eyes were wide open. He seemed to be bearing bad news.

"Why do you look so disturbed? What is the matter Kakata? Is the village under attack?" the Chief asked frantically.

"Chief, the whole village is under siege. I am afraid if you don't stand up people are going to die," said Kakata.

"Stop beating about the bush. Tell me, what went wrong?" asked Chief Kgoratau seemingly impatient.

"My Lord, everybody in the village has developed sore throat and itchy eyes. Someone must have cast a spell on us. How come the people suffer from the same disease? There can be only one explanation, witchcraft," said Kakata.

He also started coughing and rubbing his eyes which had turned blood red.

"I have just spoken to Mafahlela. He said that a witch is behind all these problems we are facing. I have ordered him to deal with the matter once and for all," said the Chief.

©PJ Ntsoane

"I hear you. Don't you think we should call the local hospital staff to send their mobile clinics to come and help us in the meantime," suggested Kakata.

"I don't think that will be necessary. This is pure witch-craft. It needs traditional doctors to deal with it. 'Motlwa o hlomolwa ka o mongwe': a thorn prick is removed with another one. Whoever are responsible for this mess will wish they were never born when I am finished with them," said Chief Kgoratau.

Kakata left the Chief sitting alone in the dark round hovel. The Chief ultimately came out of the hut and headed straight to his eldest wife's hut to have something to cheer him up. He entered the hut without knocking as always. He never knocked as he said he was the boss.

"How are you Mmakgosi? I am starving. Please give me something to eat," said Chief Kgoratau.

Mmakgosi tried to say something but no sound came out of her mouth. She could only move her lips. The Chief felt a cold shiver of fear down his spine. He asked himself what could have happened to his wife. He went to the huts of his other wives and was shocked to discover the same state of affairs in several huts. It was only his youngest wife who seemed unaffected. What immediately came to his mind was witchcraft that had engulfed his village. He went outside into the yard to have fresh air. He was met by a throng of men who burst into his court yard seemingly in exasperation. They reported that their wives had mysteriously become dumb and children caught a cold bug. He then

©PJ Ntsoane

realised that it was serious. He immediately summoned all *inyangas* (traditional doctors) to the royal court to come and solve the problems. Mafahlela was among the group of those who heeded the Chief's call. The Chief ordered them to throw their bones and identify the cause of the predicament. They all came up with the same answer: the problem was from within. The Chief became furious with the *inyangas* and Mafahlela stood up to give clarity.

"My Chief, if it may not offend you, do you still remember that you called me earlier as the head *inyanga* to help cleanse this area? All that you see as regards women who have mysteriously become dumb is the result of that cleansing. I asked you if you gave me a go ahead to curse the troublemakers and you agreed. It is very unfortunate because it cannot be undone. Whoever should try to undo this will die. All those who have that condition are the ones who have a problem with your rule," said Mafahlela.

Those who gathered there confirmed that more than half the women in the area were dumb. In a normal democracy if so many people didn't approve of a leader's governance he would be forced to abdicate. All men whose wives had become dumb became agitated. They demanded that the Chief and Mafahlela undo their curse as they could not bear to live with wives who could not communicate with them like they used to. They said that if they had been born like that they would not have a problem with their condition. Chief Kgoratau tried to justify his actions on the basis that

©PJ Ntsoane

those people wanted to topple him. The men insisted that as a Chief he was supposed to protect his subjects and not harm them.

As they were sitting there arguing, a minibus carrying the women who were arrested a day before arrived. They were accompanied by two private cars one belonging to the Chief's daughter, Kagabo. The driver of the other car was Kagabo's colleague at Lawyers for All.

He alighted from the car and went straight to the gathering. Kagabo remained with the other women.

"Greetings to you, my elders," said Leeba.

They all returned the greetings according to their culture.

"I have brought these women here to you. They are your children. As you know they were arrested here yesterday. Kagabo and I represented them and we secured bail for them. They were given free bail thanks to Kagabo's input, so we thought we should first bring them here to their Chief before they returned to their homes so that His Majesty knows that they are fine," said Leeba.

Chief Kgoratau shook his head in disbelief. Leeba felt nervous and retreated a short distance. He didn't understand why the Chief looked so furious when they had worked so hard for his subjects.

"I don't believe this. Kagabo, my eldest daughter, how could she betray me? These people are my enemies. I didn't give her education so that she would use it against me. These people want to destroy my

©PJ Ntsoane

governance, her heritage. How could she stab me in the back like this?" asked Chief Kgoratau.

"I am sorry my Lord, I will go and tell her to come and explain. We thought we were helping her people as our colleague," said Leeba running back to Kagabo and the other women.

When he arrived where they were waiting he noticed anxiety in their faces. He tried to talk to Kagabo but surprisingly she could not respond. All the other women except Malesedi could not speak. She responded to Leeba's report albeit unusually slower. Malesedi was also surprised as she could not understand as they had been singing when they entered the court yard. Leeba was forced to go back to the royal gathering with the group. They reached the gathering and were ordered to sit down. Chief Kgoratau was fuming. He called them names and blamed his daughter for betrayal.

"These people are undermining me, your own father. They threaten the security of your family. How do you justify helping these witches?" asked Chief Kgoratau.

She could not respond verbally. Malesedi was forced to come to her rescue.

"My Chief, you say all these are Malesedi's heritage. If you truly mean what you say you would recognise her as the heir to chieftaincy. The very fact that you do not think she will succeed you as the ruler of this place shows that you do not recognise her equality. By so doing you deprive her and her descendants of their heritage. She can only change that unreasonable practice if she joins the struggle for equal rights. She is

©PJ Ntsoane

your flesh and blood, and besides she is not married. Why do you doubt her capability? Isn't she educated enough? She will definitely be an asset to this community. All the natural resources given to us by God but taken away by those robbers will be restored to benefit the rightful owners. She is the only person at the moment capable of challenging those who have taken away what rightfully belongs to us. Our children's children will stand to benefit from their heritage. You need to change this oppressive old practice," said Malesedi.

"If you are not careful you will meet the same fate as your husband. He was as recalcitrant as you are right now. Where did that take him? Six feet underground. You are now a widow," said Chief Kgoratau.

Malesedi felt anger engulfing her. She tried to find words to respond to what the Chief said to her. She was lost for words for a while.

"Chief, do you know something that we don't?" asked Malesedi.

The Chief realised that he had let slip something that he thought would be a classified secret known only by the inner circle. He frowned in an attempt to cover up his embarrassment. He then tried to cancel out his error.

"I am only warning you my child. I have seen how troublesome you have become nowadays. I am only concerned that if you are not careful those who killed your husband may come for you. I know how dangerous and ruthless these people can be," said Chief Kgoratau.

©PJ Ntsoane

"If my husband was killed fighting for the rights of our people then he is a martyr. I am proud of him. Killing someone just because you happen to differ with them is not a solution. It is the worst cowardice one can ever display. Torturing or killing freedom fighters will only embolden those who believe in the course. You must go and tell them to come for me as well. I am not intimidated. If they kill me a thousand like-minded fighters will emerge. This is the struggle you will not suppress my Chief. We say: *forward ever and backward never*. The truth shall prevail and those clandestine acts will be exposed. Those responsible for evil acts will be brought to book by the real justice," said Malesedi.

"I want Kagabo to speak for herself if you say she is one of you," said Chief Kgoratau.

Kagabo tried to speak but no sound came out of her mouth. All the other women also could not utter any sound. Chief Kgoratau realised what was happening and he became afraid. His daughter had also succumbed to Mafahlela's curse. He turned to Mafahlela.

"Mafahlela, you cannot do this to the princess as well. You will have to undo your magic," said Chief Kgoratau.

"I am afraid it cannot be undone. Whoever reverses this curse will die as I have already told you. I don't want to die. You can do it yourself if you are not afraid of death. I told you when you ordered me to go ahead with the curse that the outcome would not be pleasant and you said you didn't mind as only those punished would be your enemies. Now you want to change your mind just

©PJ Ntsoane

because your loved ones are caught? You are too late my Chief," said Mafahlela.

The Chief ordered the royal security to tie up Mafahlela and lock him up in the holding bungalow until such time that he reversed his magic. Mafahlela was dragged screaming and thrown into the royal prison. Other traditional doctors tried to run away being afraid that what had befallen Mafahlela would spill over to them as well.

Chief Kgoratau ordered them to stay put. He told them to prove their salt by undoing Mafahlela's magic or they should stop practising as *inyangas* in his village as they were fraudulent.

"You are not going anywhere. You stay here in my homestead until you unravel this mystery. I am going to throw you into the dungeon like Mafahlela if you do not solve this problem. I will confiscate your pouches and you will not be seen practising as *inyangas* ever again" said Mafahlela.

Many of the *inyangas* were willing to part with their pouches if that would make them go back to their homes again. Chief Kgaratau was not willing to allow them to go.

"You have long been cheating my people with your fake medicine. Some of you have become rich from goats and cows you received as payment for your services. I am going to confiscate all your wealth. It means you have robbed my people," said Kgoratau.

The *inyangas* were on their knees and begging for mercy. They reasoned that many of their clients were

©PJ Ntsoane

from remote places as the locals regarded them as witches.

"The fact that you operated in this area with my permission and some of my subjects consulted you gives me the right to confiscate your wealth or stop you from practising here," said Chief Kgoratau.

©PJ Ntsoane

7

Sepekwa was discharged from hospital. He went straight to the Chief's kraal when he arrived at Motsetona. He looked frail but could talk. He had lost a few teeth in the assault.

"I am glad you are up and about my brother," said Chief Kgoratau.

"Thank you my Chief. God is great," he said holding his ribs to show that they were still painful.

"Did you see those who did this to you?" asked Kakata.

"No, my brother, they attacked from behind and had their faces covered. It was a bit dark and they were hiding behind a bush. They took me by surprise. Had they come from the front I would have broken their arms. I am a warrior, you know. I can't be beaten by cowards who ambush from behind. If they were real men they would have faced me rather than take me by surprise," said Sepekwa.

"Is it not because you were drunk?" asked Chief Kgoratau.

"No, I only had taken a few tots of *makhur'a sepekwa* as usual. Even if I was drunk I would have repelled them easily. I am a good fighter you know," said Sepekwa.

"What do the police say? Haven't they arrested any suspects yet?" asked Kakata.

"No. I have not heard anything yet," said Sepekwa.

"Those ones are useless my brother if I tell you. They wouldn't catch a criminal even when he committed a crime in front of them. That is why they are so overweight. All they can do best is eat, drive around and

©PJ Ntsoane

go to sleep. The government pays them for doing virtually nothing. How many cases of stock theft have we reported to them? Many of the cases reported to them have not been concluded. Even when they make arrest many of the wrong doers do not get convicted. The only cases they excel in are those of men who are arrested for teaching their arrogant and lazy wives a lesson or two," said Chief Kgoratau.

"By the way that reminds me of something that happened on that particular day," said Sepekwa.

"You know, when I was coming from the forest on that day I stumbled upon a group of women who were holding a daylight witches' meeting under that big Marula tree in the valley," said Sepekwa.

"A group of witches, did you recognise any of them?" asked Kakata.

"Yes, I know all of them. They were not aware that I was up in the tree under which they were sitting. They were let by Malesedi. I heard everything they said. My Chief if we do not stop them there will be no man left in this village. Those women are as poisonous as a black mamba to say the least," said Sepekwa.

"Tell me what I don't know. Many things happened since you were in hospital. Whatever you heard can be used against them in our royal court. They must be banished from this village before they destroy our ancestral heritage," said Kakata.

"I couldn't agree more. We need to root out these weeds before they destroy our crops," said the Chief.

©PJ Ntsoane

"My Chief, we need to call a court meeting and punish these rebels. We have Sepekwa as our witness. We have a tight case against them. Maybe they are also responsible for his attack. The police will be able to nail them if we show them that they had a reason to harm Sepekwa. They will pay for messing with our fore-fathers' ways," said Kakata.

"What do you mean? I cannot be beaten up by women. I would kill myself if ever that happened," said Sepekwa.

"No, I was only saying. I know you are a great fighter. Even a lion won't approach you. But still we can pin this incident on them just to spite them. We will have a case if you testify that they threatened you with violence after discovering that you overheard them," said Kakata.

"No ways. I am not going to humiliate myself in front of the whole world. How will people respect me when they hear that I was beaten up by a bunch of women? Please, my brother I cannot do that even if it meant getting rid of them for good," retorted Sepekwa.

The Chief paused and looked into the distance. He scratched his head. He thought deeply and took in a deep breath.

"You know I have a different approach to this nuisance. I think we should keep tabs on these troublemakers. We must know everything they do or think. We need to know how many times they took a breath or their hearts made a beat per day. We need to know how they snore and what they dream about at night when they are asleep. We could incriminate them somehow so

©PJ Ntsoane

that they are put away for good. If all fail to bear the fruits as desired, we terminate them. There are people who can do the job perfectly and they can be trusted not to link us to the crime. They have done this on several occasions and we have never seen the police snooping around," said Chief Kgoratau.

Kakata was not perplexed by the way the Chief was so rattled by these women. He knew what was at stake. He appeared desperate to solve them. Frustration was written all over his face. Their friends from overseas were beginning to ask questions. They had so much to lose as they invested billions of dollars in the projects that they ran in the area. They had made a secret pact with local authorities in return for a few favours. They gave their local friends incentives that were known by them alone. Some of these local authorities were good at pretending games that they would fool anyone that they were the victims of the system or identified with the course for justice. They spoke the language of the oppressed with so much aplomb and tenacity that the real victims would be duped into believing them. They were real chameleons that easily merged with the surroundings. It took a person with discerning eye and intelligence to pick them out.

"Maybe we should not be that brutal. I think if we could find fashionable and handsome young men to court them. They could offer a distraction. I know that women are weak when it comes to men. I think they can easily fall for any enticing young man. That way their thoughts will be preoccupied with these newly found lovers and

©PJ Ntsoane

their minds will be off track. How could they want to be involved with men stuff? This shows that they are bored with their husbands. In case of Malesedi I think she is only doing this because she is bitter after losing her husband. If she gets a new lover she will definitely cool down," said Kakata.

"That young woman is a deadly poison. I must have her banished from this area and taken far away to a place where she will not have contact with our good people. I must make sure that whenever she sets her filthy foot on my land she is arrested for trespassing. Her court case hearing is in the coming two days. We must make sure that she is found guilty of disrespecting our tradition that she is banished for real," said Kgoratau.

"You can find conviction if you want my Chief. You are the 'axe' of this community therefore whatever you decide cannot be challenged or reversed by anyone. I am only worried by her reasoning capacity and the fact that our Princess is on her side. She could incite other women to rebel if she is banished. Her influence has taken a grip in this area. She is going to be seen as the victim or a heroine if we are seen to be doing injustice to her," said Kakata.

"The last thing I desire is to turn her into a heroine. We must first demonise her so that the people in the village view her as a villain. We must be seen to have tried to be tolerant towards her and her punishment should be seen as a result of her unbearable provocation. We should make ourselves the victims in this regard. We need to have the support of her in-laws. I am sure they

©PJ Ntsoane

can be used to turn the people against her," said Sepekwa.

The men adopted the tactic used by those who want to stone a dog. They first accuse it of stealing chicken eggs and then of howling at night. They do not mention that they starved the dog until it decided to feed itself or that the howling was a result of hunger. They do not mention how many times the dog caught rabbits and how it was compensated with the intestines or a mere pat. It never got a fair share of the meat. Since the dog cannot be interviewed to hear its side of the story those who might pity it believe the executors' story.

Kagabo realised the attack she was suffering from and suspected a flu virus. She took her mother along to a medical doctor in town. The doctor examined them and drew their blood for laboratory tests. It was found that they had toxic substances in their blood samples. They were asked where that could have been contracted and they quickly remembered that the police fired a lot of teargas in the village when they were dispersing demonstrators. Since the village is in a low humid valley the presence of the toxic gas could not be cleared quickly or else the police used banned chemicals to disperse them. The people in the village were seemingly allergic to the chemicals. Kagabo quickly notified the officials of the Health and Environmental Department who dispatched workers to the area to do tests and check those who displayed symptoms associated with inhalation of toxic gas. Indeed, the officials discovered

©PJ Ntsoane

shocking evidence. It was not only the gas used by the police. Emissions from fertilizer and mining companies in the area had contributed to pollution of the environment. Kagabo decided to institute a court case for compensation of the victims of the activities of the companies in the area. First she called social groups in the area including Malesedi's to raise funds to tackle the mighty companies. Her father was riled by his daughter's decision and tried to dissuade her from taking on those multinational companies.

"My child I want to advise you as your father that you should stop trying to investigate these companies. I don't think they could be responsible. These people are very educated so there is no way they will produce anything that will put the lives of the people at risk. They conducted feasibility research in the area before commencement of production. Besides they have created jobs for our people. Their lease created income for this royal house as well. They also gave you and many other children from our area bursaries to study at different universities in the country and abroad. Some of the beneficiaries from this area are now millionaires working overseas. Please my child I love you so much I don't want to lose you. These people can be very dangerous. They wouldn't hesitate to eliminate you if they feel that you are in their way. Please my daughter I am begging you, stop this," said Chief Kgoratau.

"Dad, I am sorry. My conscience does not allow me to let go of this matter. There is so much at stake here. My people's health and our God given environment need

©PJ Ntsoane

protection. If we the young ones do not stand up, our children's children will find nothing left. Who are they going to blame for that? Do you think they are going to blame the foreign nationals and their multinational companies? No dad, they are going to blame those who allowed those foreign nationals to come here and destroy their heritage. Those foreign nationals are only here to make money. They don't care about the welfare of local people. They produce false reports and give us those few bursaries you are talking about to convince people like you to think that they have our interests at heart. They cannot do this to their own communities. Do you know why? It is because they think their lives are more valuable. Our people cannot grow anything around here themselves. If you don't do anything about this Dad, History will judge you harshly. I want to be remembered by the coming generations as the one who stood up for the rights of her people. The one who died for the betterment of the conditions of her people and their heritage if ever I get killed as you have just said," said Kagabo.

Chief Kgoratau couldn't believe what he heard. He suddenly looked away outside the window. He had tears in his eyes that he didn't want his daughter to notice. He knew if he couldn't convince his daughter to change her mind she would end up like the rest who made the hit list. He was in the circle of ruthless murderers who would stop at nothing to achieve their objectives. He realised that his daughter had inherited his bravery and stubbornness. He saw himself in the fire displayed in her

©PJ Ntsoane

eyes when she was convinced of a just course she had to carry out. His wife who had been listening to their conversation without intervening decided to have a say in the matter.

"I think your father is right in this case. Listen to what he says as he has experience. Do you think he would mislead you?" asked Mmakgosi.

"Ma, I don't doubt my father's intelligence. It is just that in this instance he is wrong and I am right," said Kagabo.

"No my child, look at you, a qualified lawyer on account of these people's bursary. The beautiful suits that your father and all members of Motsetona Tribal Council wear are donated by these foreign companies. The cars that they drive were donated by them. The local leaders are entitled to an all costs paid holiday trip abroad once a year. We, as the royal family, are guaranteed shares in the enterprises operating here. As your father has said, they have the interests of this community at heart. You need to have a positive attitude. The gas leakage could have been an accident that eluded them," Mmakgosi said.

"No Mama, these people give you these suits and all the stuff to tie you up or silence you. I will not be black-mailed into silence when I can make a difference. They helped me yes, I appreciate that. But that does not force me to keep quiet or turn a blind eye when I see injustice being visited upon my people by my so-called helpers. I am afraid I am going to have to disappoint you there as I won't back down," said Kagabo.

©PJ Ntsoane

Chief Kgoratau received a message on his cellphone inviting him to an emergency meeting of the members of The Social Council. It consisted of local chiefs, members of the ruling political party and representatives of companies that do business in the area. He quickly summoned his driver and a few elders to accompany him to the seemingly urgent meeting.

When he arrived at the venue he found several other local leaders already there. They were busy enjoying snacks and drinks to while away time while waiting for the rest of the members to arrive. Their laughter, triggered by flimsy jokes was so loud that one would think the roof of the conference hall where they were meeting would be blown off. As Chief Kgoratau entered the conference hall those in there suddenly fell silent and stared at him as if seeing an intruder. He felt as if their eyes pierced through his soul and he became a little embarrassed. He wondered what that was all about but could sense heavy tension. He greeted those gathered and they mumbled in response. Some turned away from him.

The meeting was attended by business magnates from the East who only flew in whenever there was a serious issue to discuss. They were dressed in their elegant corporate designer suits and wearing expensive crocodile skin shoes. Their watches were worth millions of dollars when put together. Their regalia looked so expensive that one could smell millions of dollars enough to feed the whole country. The Social Council

©PJ Ntsoane

members' suits were nowhere near those worn by the executives from abroad. All aspired to have possession of those symbols of prosperity. They could lay their hands on those only if they toed the line drawn by their bosses.

When all were present the chairperson of the council declared the meeting officially opened. The first to speak was the Paramount King Tau. He was the one whom the foreign enterprises entrusted with power over their local social investment projects. He was wearing a snow white suit, a white pure silk shirt, a red tie, a leopard skin hat and cape.

"Dear members, as you already know we have a serious challenge posed by forces of destruction who want to scupper development in this area. These people have found leverage in the recent accidental emissions that affected people in the valley. They are threatening to close investments made by our friends from foreign countries on the basis that their industrial activities pollute the environment. We all know that these people have always been troublesome. We have tried to douse their fires of anti-development but it seems the embers are setting the forest alight again. Unfortunately those elements are the progeny of some members here and also beneficiaries of the goodwill of the very foreign investors. I wonder why our members fail to drive sense into the heads these elements. I am not the one to beat about the bush. I will always be frank when a need arises. I want members to tell this Council their experiences and how they are going to bring this

©PJ Ntsoane

nuisance to a stop. There is so much at stake here, we cannot afford to slip or lose focus. These friends of ours have done us a great favour by coming here and choosing to invest their money in the development of our area. They could as well have chosen to build their businesses in other areas. So we need to play our role of establishing an enabling ground for our mutual success," said King Tau.

The business magnates were nodding their heads occasionally when the King mentioned something that was pleasant to their ears. All local members of The Social Council explained their experiences and showed how they promoted the interest of the Council in their respective areas of jurisdiction.

Chief Kgoratau was the last to speak. One could hear a pin drop as all paid attention to what he had to say.

"My King, friends from abroad and fellow members of the council, I am the one who rules the area that seems to be the eye of the storm. My council of elders and I are doing everything in our power to douse the flames of insurrection. We know who the inciters are and we promise this Council that we have everything under control. The culprits are not the people we cannot sway if we push a little bit harder. I promise you that when we disperse from here we are going to clean up the mess for good. I also call upon other members to help extinguish bonfires in their areas because if they don't we will not effectively root out the trouble. Unrest is not entirely in my area. It has already spread to other villages around. You must know that these people are

©PJ Ntsoane

very educated and know how to mobilise support. We need to reinforce our campaign," said Chief Kgoratau.

"My Chief you cannot surely fail to control your own children. You gave birth to these people. You need to stamp your authority as the head of the family or their ruler. Don't you know the saying that: *'Go nyatsa kgosi ke go tloga'*- If you disobey the king you will be banished. Make that practicable," said King Tau.

The king was saying that based on African tradition that traditional rulers are called, *'Beng mabu'*- literally translated it means owners of the land. If a king or a chief died people would say: *'Mobu o utswitswe'*- meaning the soil has been stolen. This confers upon the traditional ruler a false impression that he can do whatever he pleases with the land and the subjects will not object. These chiefs sell and lease the land to foreign companies and local investors without proper consultation with their subjects. This tendency is contrary to the African saying that: *'kgoši ke kgoši ka batho'* which literally means a king or chief rules according to the will of the people. It translates that the King or chief is accountable to the subjects. It also entails that there has to be consultation before any major decision pertaining to communal affairs is taken.

The meeting ended and business friends from abroad gave each member a paper bag full of expensive gifts and clothing vouchers. Some of the presents were made of the by-products of resources mined in the area. The recipients were so enticed by the glittering trinkets that

©PJ Ntsoane

they wore smiles on their faces. They promised to leave no stone unturned to root out troublemakers from their otherwise loyal subjects.

©PJ Ntsoane

7

8

The Central Committee of the Social Council decided to stage their ultimate campaign to eliminate those who wanted to disturb development in the area in the name of environmental issues. One member who was known to be a political demagogue and an executive member of Mahala Party that governed the municipalities in the area was a guest speaker at a local radio station. He launched a tirade against the activists who were described as anti-revolutionaries and opportunists who were undesirable.

"You see comrades, there is no foreign investor who can come and invest his money in a country where there is high risk of a loss. These anti-revolutionaries are destroying our hope of eradicating unemployment and under-development in our area. We are bound to engage them by any means necessary. It doesn't matter if it becomes messy. By the way the end justifies the means. We cannot allow a few misguided individuals to hold the majority to ransom," said Pistol. He was nicknamed Pistol because whenever he talked about something that involved political contestation he would position his fingers like he was holding a handgun. He would punctuate his speech with the imitation of a gun being fired.

The social activists on the other hand wanted their communities to have a stake in the profits made by the companies by being granted communal shares. They demanded that those displaced by the investors be

©PJ Ntsoane

proportionately compensated by sustainable job offers and workers' shares for having lost their means of livelihood. They also demanded that those companies that produce toxic emissions be shut down and in their place introduce those that produce environmentally friendly products. They called their campaign a fight for true corporate citizenship.

Malesedi persuaded Kagabo to institute litigation against those involved in the contracts that harmed the people's lives. They formed a committee that made forensic investigations into the contracts signed. Kagabo was shocked to find that the traditional rulers and councilors in the area were involved in underhand dealings with these foreign companies. Her conscience didn't allow her to abandon the case. She was aware of the dangers involved if she pursued the case. Her resolve to do justice for the helpless people in the villages was unshaken by the possible consequences. They enlisted the services of NGOs from the West which promoted human rights. They helped with fund raising for their legal battles. The NGOs were so amenable to the women's course that they pumped in several thousands of dollars into the Concerned Women's Committee (CWC) bank account. An attempt by The Social Council to institute prohibitory bureaucracy was wittily brushed aside by NGO leaders who were very adept in that regard.

The day set for Malesedi's royal court hearing finally dawned. All the elders of her family and her in-laws were present. They were asked to state their cases

©PJ Ntsoane

respectively. Surprisingly Malesedi was allowed to speak standing up like the men did. Chief Kgoratau didn't want to adjourn the hearing any further. She had to be removed. Her pleas would only be a formality. He felt his blood boiling when he saw her addressing the court on her feet.

"My Chief and elders, I have nothing against traditional practices. The only reason why I do not want to perform the rituals is because I am a born-again Christian. My husband was also a born-again Christian. In fact he was the one who converted me to this religion. I loved my husband with all my heart. I know that where he is in Heaven, he is supporting me in the stance I have taken. He would not be happy to see me mourn him the way my in-laws want me to. He wouldn't want me to be laden with sad memory of his passing for a long twelve months. He would want me to move on and be happy. I know he would only want me to have sweet memory of the best moments we spent together. Now my elders want me to shave my head and wear a black cloak as a sign of being a widow. To make matters worse they want me to strip naked for another man chosen by my in-laws so that he smears the *muti* (herbs) mixed in the blood of a goat. That is against my religion. My husband was the only man who ever saw me naked and I hope it remains so until I go to my grave. I beg you to soften your hearts and allow me to live my life the way I wish to. It is not snubbing of my elders and old tradition. It is just that things have changed," said Malesedi sitting down slowly. There was silence in the court yard.

©PJ Ntsoane

Everybody was staring at Malesedi in amazement. Some women who were allowed to attend as witnesses were envying her bravery while others were appalled.

"We have heard the closing arguments by Malesedi. I would allow the plaintiff to state their final argument, if any, before the Chief gives his final verdict," said Kakata. Then Matobe stood up to talk. He looked pale due to fatigue.

"Thank you my Chief, all I wanted to say has been said. I can only say that I am your loyal servant and will be content with your wise judgment," said Matobe.

Then Chief Kgoratau cleared his throat and waved his whisk of a lion's tail hair. He kept quiet for a moment which seemed like eternity. People, especially men, were anxious to hear how the woman who disrespected the people's culture was punished so severely that others would be taught a lesson.

"My people, it pains me to see my children in conflict over a matter that makes us who we are as a people. We have become a laughing stock of other people as we do not respect ourselves. How do we expect other nations to respect us? They will only rejoice when they see us at each other's throat over trifles like the one we are gathered to discuss here today. I have travelled the whole world and have never seen people in those countries disrespect themselves. It only happens with us, Africans. It doesn't take much trouble for our enemies to stir disturbance amongst us. They only need to look from a distance and laugh in order for us to finish each other off. We, the elderly, need to be

©PJ Ntsoane

custodians of our identity. We must protect our culture with everything we have. Remember those who want to humiliate us can only succeed if we abet their activities. What message are we sending if we fold our arms or only shrug our shoulders?

Now I have arrived at my decision on this matter. I have observed how our daughter here behaved during the hearing and attentively listened to what she said. I have also heard the statements of the plaintiffs. It is not in my nature to sow strife or fan trouble in families. I would rather see peace prevail because families are the nucleus of our tribe. If we have a tribe where homes are divided we won't have a united nation. That is why I call upon every individual to make it their own business to promote our moral values all the time. I have thought long and hard about this matter. This is a very sensitive and an unusual case as you can see. It is common knowledge that our culture does not allow a widow to divorce the dead. But given the merits of this case, I have decided that the Matobes should be reimbursed the bridal price they paid to the Balepes when they married their daughter. It is only fair because their daughter has not given the Matobes any heirs nor filled their kraal. She still stands the chance of being married into other families to redeem their loss. All dismissed," said Chief Kgoratau.

He stood up and all were on their feet to allow the Chief to disappear into the royal huts. The people started filing out of the court yard murmuring all sorts of opinions.

©PJ Ntsoane

Malesedi advised her elders to appeal the decision of the Chief at the royal court higher than that of Motsetona. Paramount King Tau was above Chief Kgoratau. He had the powers to overrule decisions taken by the subordinate chiefs. An application was made for the Paramount King to hear the matter.

King Tau set up a date for the hearing of Malesedi's appeal. On that day Kakata, Sepekwa, Lerumo and many other men from Motsetona attended as they had interest in the case. The men felt that Malesedi had weakened their authority as heads of their families as a result of the teachings she gave to their wives. In their eyes she was undesirable, but to the wives she was a heroine who opened their eyes and minds. She was a God-sent. They felt like the children of Israel liberated from slavery in Babylon. Even though they had not yet arrived in Canaan, all their hopes were in the success of Malesedi. Her failure and humiliation would signify a reversion to oppression. They put her in their prayers every day. Some men were already gloating about Malesedi's defeat saying that it was a lesson to the recalcitrant women not to challenge the laws set by God at creation. Whenever men seemed triumphant the women would begin to doubt the logic behind their struggle for equality and socio-economic emancipation. Some of them were consoled by the hardships that the children of Israel had to go through before they reached the Promised Land. They would tell those who wore smug smiles on their faces to enjoy it while it lasted.

©PJ Ntsoane

However, the faint hearted women among them deserted the struggle.

It was the day of the appeal hearing at King Tau's court. There was a case that had to be heard before Malesedi's. It was brought by a man called Njeleng who wanted his neighbour and friend Modiri to pay damages for having seduced his wife while he was away working in the city. Njeleng claimed that Modiri had violated his personality by invading his homestead when he impregnated his wife.

"My King, I feel demeaned by that man. I went to the city to work for my wife and children so that they would have a better life. That man, Modiri wormed himself into my wife's heart and violated her. He disrespected my honour and family dignity. I want him to restore my human dignity," said Njeleng.

Modiri was ordered by Mmoledi, the court interpreter to defend himself.

"Your Majesty, Njeleng has admitted that I am not only his neighbour but also an old friend. Before he left for the big city he came to me and asked me to look after his livestock and family during his absence. He said he trusted me as a good friend and what was his was mine. He said his cows should not be burned by milk in their udders while I was there to relieve them by filling his children's buckets with it. He also said to me that I should kill the snakes in his homestead while he was away. He even said that I should help his wife with whatever she might ask for and promised to pay me back when he returned. My Lord, I did not force myself

©PJ Ntsoane

on her. She was the one who called me one night to come and kill a snake that had entered her hut," said Modiri.

"You went there at night to kill a snake? How did you receive the message? Mmoledi asked.

"She called me on my cellphone. She sounded agitated. I had to rush in and help my friend's wife as he had asked me to. I didn't want to let my friend down. By the way a promise is a promise," retorted Modiri.

"And tell us what happened next," said Mmoledi.

"I killed the snake my Lord. And what a big and dangerous snake it was! There was no way my friend's wife could have killed it alone," said Modiri.

"What happened next?" Mmoledi asked.

"My friend's wife was in a state of shock as she was crying hysterically. I had to comfort her. I held her in my arms and she was crying on my chest. She asked me to hold her tightly as she felt safe in my arms. My Lord, I didn't want to, but she was my friend's wife and she needed my help. I had promised my friend to do anything for his family as he had asked. If my friend's wife needed me to squeeze her I had no option but to do as she asked since she was crying. She was tense initially and she slowly became limp in my arms. She was panting heavily and I could feel her heart beat pounding against my chest. Then she raised her lips towards mine and kissed me. I let go of her but she begged me not to go as she was afraid to be alone because the children were already asleep," said Modiri. Njeleng could not take it anymore. He leaped from his

©PJ Ntsoane

stool and went for Modiri's throat. He was fuming. They wrestled. He wanted to squeeze life out of Modiri. Court guards found it hard to separate the two men who were exchanging fists like heavy-weight world championship boxers. It took eight strong men to dislodge the vice-grips of the two men and ultimately restrain them. Modiri managed to head-butt Njeleng on his lips and eye. He was bleeding in the mouth and his eye was swollen. People thought that he had lost his front teeth because he spit out a thick blood clot.

The court elders then immediately continued with deliberations on the issue. They asked questions in an attempt to solve the case. Some asked if it was right to blame someone for keeping the promise he had made to his friend. They maintained that Njeleng did not tell his friend the boundaries he didn't have to cross. They said that since he had asked his friend to do everything for his family what his wife asked qualified in exact sense of the word.

Others maintained that women were gullible and vulnerable like children would be, therefore, Njeleng as a man was expected to have exercised restraint in that situation. Then it was time for the King to give his verdict.

"I have heard your versions both of you. I have also heard other members' inputs in this matter. I have now come to a conclusion. First of all I am not happy with the way Njeleng behaved here today. You have proved beyond reasonable doubt that you cannot contain your temper. Things done in anger are often regretted. I have

©PJ Ntsoane

no choice but to slap you with a fine of two goats. You have disrespected this court by attacking a man in our presence. You had no business in doing that. You need to pay this man a goat as well for the bruises he suffered. This is irrespective of the blood and tooth you have shed.

As for the accused I have decided to teach everyone in this village that a man does not defile the bed of another one while he is still alive. You will have to pay this man and his family the number of cows he paid to his wife's family as dowry. I understand that Njeleng paid ten cows, five goats and ten sheep for his wife's hand in marriage. That is according to our wedding records. Remember we keep record of every marriage settlement here at the royal kraal. So we know exactly what we are talking about. You have betrayed the trust of your friend. Njeleng will not have to worry about going back to the big city to work. You will make sure that he gets whatever he was getting at his place of employment. Therefore let this be a lesson to all who run around in the cover of the night worming into the beds of other men and defiling their women. We have high respect for family integrity as the foundation of our nation. Those who violate families are declaring war against us. They will be dealt with accordingly. Our court is the custodian of good morals," said King Tau.

All who gathered there sang praises and wished their king a long life so that they would continue benefitting from his wisdom. They concluded their singing with a call to the ancestors to bless them with torrents of rain

©PJ Ntsoane

and plenty of harvest. The court took a short break for the King to refresh for the next case.

The case that followed was that of Malesedi's appeal against Chief Kgoratau's verdict. Malesedi was the first to state her argument and Kakata spoke on behalf of Chief Kgoratau. The Chief felt it was beneath him to appear with his subject himself.

The King gave his final say on the matter. His decision was final and no other traditional court could challenge him. The parties in the case were expected to abide by the decision however painful it might be. The only court that could be approached to overrule his decision was the Constitutional Court, the highest court in the land. No one had ever taken that route before. All complied with his judgment without further complaint.

"I listened carefully to what the complainant and the accused said on the matter. Here is my final decision. This decision should be regarded objectively. It is without favour or prejudice. I hereby declare, according to the powers bestowed upon me by God and ancestors of this land, that the decision taken by my subordinate Chief Kgoratau was reasonable given the merits of the case. I uphold his decision categorically. Case dismissed," thus concluded Paramount King Tau.

All men from Motsetona roared in appreciation of the King's decision not to overturn Chief Kgoratau's verdict. Malesedi felt numbness overpowering her. The King's maintenance of Chief Kgoratau's verdict meant that she had been disinherited. She no longer had a home of her

©PJ Ntsoane

own. She was no longer regarded as the daughter-in-law of the Matobes.

One day when she was at work the police came looking for her. They budged into her office and arrested her. She was told that she was charged with attempted murder and grievous bodily harm. This related to Sepekwa's case. She was framed for the crime in an attempt to discredit her and frustrate her efforts to challenge the traditional rulers in the area as well as those who had made business deals with local leaders. She was seen as a threat because of her activities. Fortunately Kagabo happened to have come to pay her a visit when all those things happened. She followed them to the police station. She immediately applied for bail which was granted. She could otherwise have spent the night in the police holding cells.

When Chief Kgoratau heard about what she did for Malesedi, he reprimanded her for continuing to help his enemies. She was surprised because even King Tau called her trying to persuade her to stop interfering. She asked him how helping her clients would be regarded as interference. When she asked him if he had anything to do with framing Malesedi he only said she had to stay clear of the raging wild fire as the flames would scald her.

©PJ Ntsoane

9

Malesedi could not return to her in-laws' village as she had been declared a *persona non grata* by the traditional courts. She headed to her parents' home. All villagers regarded a woman who was expelled from her in-laws or divorced as a pariah. They gossiped about her and hollered in laughter whenever they saw her. No woman wanted to be associated with her. For a few days she was a loner. The only person who paid her a visit was Princess Kagabo who advised her to take the matter to the Constitutional Court. Malesedi was not interested since she was a career woman. She felt she could look after herself regardless. She looked for accommodation in the nearest town where she was working. She was fortunate to find a house the previous owners of which had relocated to Johannesburg. It had been on the market for a while so the property agency was able to secure her a temporary occupation while they processed the papers.

One day, while on her way home after paying her parents a visit, a huge truck appeared from a steep hill and drove straight towards her. If she had not swerved her car quickly she would have been overrun. She only veered off the road and her car was brought to a stop by a large sand dune. The truck didn't stop but honked a hooter and sped off. She was very shocked and wondered if the driver was playful or it was her enemies trying to scare her off. All these made her feel more determined because she could see that her enemies

©PJ Ntsoane

were disturbed by her actions. She was convinced that all that showed they were running out of options or desperate. She referred to them as cornered foxes.

Malesedi and members of the Concerned Women's Committee used the funds they received from the human rights NGOs to establish several projects aimed at empowering women on matters pertaining to adult education, family planning, agricultural cooperatives, HIV/AIDS awareness, breast and cervical cancer awareness, vocational training, and political awareness. Traditional leaders and members of the ruling party viewed their activities with suspicion. They tried to infiltrate and destabilise them without success. The women threatened the comfort zone of their patriarchal bureaucracy. If they weren't stopped they would derail their gravy train. Several of the women were incriminated in petty crimes like possession of drugs. The drugs were planted in their homes and police staged flimsy searches on frivolous reasons of having received a tip-off. These people were so desperate to discourage and intimidate the women by following some of them even when they went shopping in the supermarkets in town and slipping items into their pockets or handbags in order to have them arrested. Kagabo became very busy helping these women comrades to win their court battles. Her father hated what she was doing for her comrades and tried without success to stop her. He regretted sending her to school to study law. He wished she had followed teaching or

©PJ Ntsoane

nursing as a career. He remembered that he was the one who insisted on her following law as a career. She reluctantly agreed to study law. He thought her legal expertise would help him entrench his position in the businesses operating in the area. Foreign companies were queuing for deals to invest in their place as it was imbued with precious natural resources that required exploitation by highly skilled multinational companies.

King Tau and the Mayor had a secret meeting as the top leaders. They wanted to bring to a halt the problem that was destabilising their area.

"Mr. Mayor, we need to take care of these troublesome flies. They have long been making noise near our ears. They can't see reason therefore they have to be terminated for good," said King Tau.

"I couldn't agree with you more. We need to take these flies out of the milk. Ultimate solution is necessary. We need to tread warily though. If we take one wrong turn we could muddy the waters. We need to find perfect executors to carry out the jobs. They must look like accidents so that the people will not suspect anything," said the Mayor.

"Yeah, this time around we do not include Kgoratau since his daughter is the target. We gave him enough time to solve the problem amicably but he has failed thus far. He has shown that he is not the bull of the kraal. Let us do the work for him," said King Tau.

The two plotters hired the services of an assassin who had never disappointed. He sneaked into Chief

©PJ Ntsoane

Kgoratau's kraal one cloudy and dark night. There was a menacing thunderstorm approaching from the south-west. Everybody had scurried to the shelter of their places of abode. Even jackals that usually roamed the night could be hardly heard. There was an uneasy calm that preceded every storm. The sound of an owl could be heard piercing the ears of scared children who always hid under their beds whenever there was lightning and thunder. Children would always wonder why God brought a scary rain when they could only have a calm drizzle. Hailstorms destroyed their parents' crops in the fields and turned their beautiful wall decorations into ruins. They hated these hazardous rains and always said short prayers asking God to stop their onslaught.

Kagabo had come home that night because she wanted to spend some time with her mother. She had parked her car outside in the yard as always. She didn't like parking it in the garage. There was security in the royal homestead so she didn't think it was necessary.

The assassin Hoezit, tampered with the brakes of Kagabo's car. He wanted her to have an accident while driving on a winding down hill road where she had to use the brakes often. The following morning her father wanted to rush to town to attend to personal issues and also to see the King thereafter. When he got into his car he found that its fuel level was very low. It was not enough to cover the long distance to town or nearest filling station. He asked his daughter if she could allow his men to tap out fuel from her car. Kagabo didn't

©PJ Ntsoane

intend to go anywhere that day as she was on leave. She allowed her father to use her car instead. The Chief was so glad to use his daughter's car since it was a brand new import. He was smiling when he climbed in the back passenger sit. His driver revved the German machine and sped off. They drove for several kilometres until they came to a curve that was downhill. The brakes of the car failed to grip and the car rolled over and plunged into a cliff. Some drivers who were following the car saw what happened, they immediately stopped to help the injured and also called the rescue team that rushed them to the nearest hospital. Chief Kgoratau's driver passed away the following day. The Chief was flown to a better equipped hospital in Gauteng Province. He had suffered severe head injuries so he needed expert surgeons who could not be flown out of the province due to costs involved and the facilities required to perform the job thoroughly. Patients from all over the world sought their services since they were the best.

Chief Kgoratau remained in intensive care for three months since he was in coma. The elders of Motsetona kept his condition a secret. They didn't want to press the panic button and risk a chaotic situation. According to African tradition a tribe is not supposed to be without a leader. Kakata was appointed by the elders to manage the affairs of the tribe in the interim. He was the obvious choice since he was the second son of the late Chief. He deputised Chief Kgoratau. In case anything happened to the Chief and rendered him incapacitated,

©PJ Ntsoane

a regent would be appointed. Women were not afforded the same rights. If a chief died without a male heir, his younger brothers would take over according to their seniority or bear a son who would ultimately ascend the throne.

Malesedi somehow heard about what happened to the Chief and offered her sympathy to her friend Kagabo. She mentioned to her that she suspected criminal acts in what happened to the Chief.

"You know my friend I suspect a baleful attempt on your father's life or yours. I personally regard what happened to me on the road a day before this accident involving your father, when a truck veered from its lane and came towards me, as a planned assassination attempt. The car your father was traveling in was yours. Those people didn't really want to hurt your father. That was aimed at you. I am saying this because you have been helping those persecuted by the system. You helped the women when they were arrested. You are a member of the CWC and serve in the committees of several women emancipation formations. You are fighting for the rights of the dispossessed masses. In fact you are a threat to the establishment of patriarchy and social evils. It would therefore be befitting to be regarded as a threat and then a target. Those people are dangerous Kagabo. They have killed many people including my darling husband. Those people will stop at nothing. Your father might not have been aware of the planned hit against you since they knew he would not approve of elimination of his own flesh and blood," said Malesedi.

©PJ Ntsoane

"No my friend you are reading too much into this," said Kagabo. She felt a little bit uneasy though. She remembered what her father used say about those who owned businesses in the area. She began to develop second thoughts about her complacency but did not want to show.

"Believe what you may, but I am telling you this was not a mere accident. We need to be careful from now on. The other freedom fighters need to be made aware of the tactics employed by the enemy," said Malesedi.

"Of course, you are right my friend. Precautionary measures are important when engaged in war. Anything is possible. We are challenging greedy people's rapacity by demanding equal share of the golden eggs laid by our God given goose," said Kagabo.

On her way home Malesedi was pursued by a suspicious car with dimmed windows. She tried to shake it off but could not because the road did not have much traffic. She drove passed a road leading to her new home and sped to the police station. The suspicious car sped off when the occupants realised she had entered a police station. She tried to open a case against the stalkers but the warrant officer refused on the basis that there was no evidence to support what she was saying. He promised to investigate the matter and be on the lookout for the car as described by Malesedi. Malesedi left the police station after a futile attempt to ask the police to escort her back home. The police stated that they didn't have enough vehicles at the station.

©PJ Ntsoane

"You don't even have officers who are patrolling the neighbourhood. That is why criminals do as they please in this area. You are wasting taxpayers' money by sitting here idling and cracking stupid jokes. One can hear your foolish laughter miles away. When law abiding citizens ask for your help it is not forthcoming. If I could go into the township I would definitely find a police car parked at an officer's girlfriend's place," said Malesedi.

"You must be careful of what you are saying Madam. We can open a case against you right now and lock you up. You can't come here to insult us. I am going to close my eyes when I open them I must find you gone otherwise I lock you up," said the Warrant Officer.

One police officer teased her with comments that she should find herself a man to protect her otherwise he would be willing to be of assistance in that regard.

"I find your comments offensive to say the least. That is disrespectful and unethical. I am going away but be warned that should anything happen to me I am going to sue you," said Malesedi.

The officers at the station burst in laughter. They said how could a person who was afraid of a whiz of wind stand up to them. They ridiculed her claim of being stalked. She left the police station disappointed. She vowed to contest elections one day. She promised to bring those arrogant and irresponsible officers to book when she was in government.

She arrived at home only to find that someone had broken into her house. Her television set, DVD player, expensive camera and her jewellery box were missing.

©PJ Ntsoane

The whole house was ransacked. She called the same police station to report the matter. The same police officers who had insulted her earlier came to investigate.

"Now I hope you will believe me when I say there are people out to harm me. If this is not enough evidence then I don't know what would make you believe, maybe my corpse," Malesedi said angrily.

The police officers looked at each other feeling a little embarrassed.

"Don't worry, madam. We will leave no stone unturned to bring those who are responsible for this act to book. This is a crime scene now. You need to find an alternative accommodation so that you do not disturb the evidence. We have to cordon off this house. Do you have anyone who will stay with you for the night or anywhere you can go for the night?" the officer asked.

"No. I have no one who can come over this time of the night. You must leave one of the officers to guard my home for the night. I will sleep in the back room tonight," Malesedi suggested.

"That won't be necessary Madam. Our experience tells us that the criminals won't be returning to this scene anytime soon. They know that we are here and cannot risk being arrested," said the officer.

"That is the experience that made you ridicule my suggestion earlier on that there were people following me I guess. I don't know if I should trust that experience of yours this time around. I will see what I can do to protect myself while you still figure out how to do your

©PJ Ntsoane

job very well. I am afraid I can't trust your judgment, Mr. Officer. Once bitten twice shy," Malesedi quipped.

"We cannot force you to do anything. All you need to know is we are not presently in a position to offer you special protection without a court order to that effect. But we will make sure that our guys patrol this area from now on," the Officer said.

"Yeah right, just like they had been doing when the criminals were breaking into my house or when I was being chased by those rogues," Malesedi sneered.

Malesedi realised that she had to protect herself in the absence of state protection. She recruited the services of a security company run by a woman. She didn't trust men anymore. Their condescending attitude sent shivers down her spine. She wouldn't risk putting her life in the hands of those who undermined her kind. The company assigned their best guards who had reputation as astute shooters. She also had done training on handling guns before. She took out her gun and carried it in the pocket of her jacket regularly. She visited a shooting range time and again to sharpen her shooting skills. The more she was surrounded by bodyguards the more she felt unsafe.

Concerned Women's Club decided to register a political party to contest the coming municipal elections. Their party manifesto was based on enforced corporate citizenship, gender equity and locals' shares in the companies that did business in their area. Their manifesto sent alarm waves to those who prospered in

©PJ Ntsoane

the illicit activities of foreign companies. They regarded the party as a threat that had to be denied platform. Their rivals intensified their mudslinging campaign to discredit members of the Social Inclusive Party (SIP). Men who were members were labeled as sissies who allowed women to dictate terms to them. The men were targeted and ridiculed openly wherever there was a social gathering. The battles were taken to their places of work. People were recruited and paid to insult them so that they would lose temper. Many of the members were arrested for various crimes including assault.

"We need to make lives of members of this new party a living hell. We are in charge here. There is no way we are going to let new comers upset us. We'll fight them with all we have. I am only disturbed by their political gatherings. They draw large crowds and that does not augur well for our mission. They seem to have a magnet that pulls these people to them," said the Mayor.

"I need to issue a decree that those who attend these meetings shall be charged with treason against their King. And they know that punishment for that is severe since they will be uprooted. No one would like to be banished. It's too drastic a punishment to dare. Malesedi survived because she is educated and employed by that NGO from the West. If she was employed by the government we would have had her dismissed using our connections. There are very few people who are that lucky," King Tau said.

The King acted on his promise and issued a decree threatening those who attended Social Inclusive Party's

©PJ Ntsoane

meetings with banishment from the area under his jurisdiction. Every chief and *Induna* (headman) was told to deal with those who defied the order harshly.

The threats made SIP very popular because the people saw them as victims of royal and bureaucratic arrogance. Majority regarded the party as their mouthpiece since the traditional leaders and their councils discriminated against those who were not of royal blood. It didn't matter how educated you were, if you were not a descendant of the ruling family your opinion was never considered. You would be called *molata or mohlanka* (servant) regardless. The people wanted change. Malesedi and Kagabo filled the vacuum of leadership for the voiceless and the disempowered. Malesedi was the one who was most visible as a spokesperson. She was a good orator. Crowds ate out of her hand whenever she addressed them. She helped launch social clubs which served as vehicles to inspire people about the new course that they had to fight for. They saw in her a brave freedom fighter who could free them from their bondage. The young and old whispered her name and ideas wherever they met.

One rainy night Malesedi's parents were attacked by criminals. They assaulted and tied up everybody in the homestead and set the huts alight. In one of the burned huts there was a three year old baby who was asleep. The attackers didn't see her when they dragged out the others and tied them up in one of the huts left intact. Their intention was to scare them so that Malesedi would realise that if she didn't stop fueling dissent in

©PJ Ntsoane

the area her loved ones would be hurt. When the people in the community saw the blaze they came out in numbers to try to rescue the people and salvage whatever items they could. Initially they thought that the homestead was struck by lightning as there was thunder. They heard the screams of those tied up in the hut. They were quickly untied and they joined villagers who were trying to extinguish the raging fires. Malesedi's cousin remembered that her child was asleep in one of the rooms that were already nearly razed to the ground. She cried hysterically and called on the people to rescue her child but it was too little too late.

The news of the attack reached Malesedi who rushed to the scene. The tragedy was in the news media all over the world. Sympathy came from all corners of the earth. The local leaders, the police and the national government condemned the cowardly act and as always promised to leave no stone unturned to bring the criminals to book. That was what they harped on like parrots whenever there was a crisis. They called it public relations. They would say all sorts of promises for the media to portray them as concerned. Everything would be forgotten thereafter. The King offered to bury the dead baby and the municipality promised to bring temporary shelter in the form of tents for the bereaved family. Malesedi convinced her parents to reject the help from the King and local municipality on the basis that they were the main suspects in those dastardly acts. Instead she accepted help from Human Rights

©PJ Ntsoane

NGOs operating in the area. They built new houses for Malesedi's family members. The houses were even more beautiful and spacious than those destroyed by the criminals. The houses were so unique in the area that they became the envy of many people in the village who naively wished the tragedy had befallen them. They forgot how painful it was for Malesedi and her relatives who had lost their loved one.

©PJ Ntsoane

10

"It is done my King. The weakest link has been fixed. He has now joined the ancestors. I feel so terrible, spilling my own blood," said Kakata.

"Don't worry. You did what had to be done. Chief Kgoratau was too weak to protect our interests. He could not deal with his own daughter and that little witch Malesedi. They have now become a nuisance in this area. It is fate because when you are in charge we cannot have this nonsense going on. Our ancestors gave us these riches to use them the way we want. We have freedom to choose who we share them with. We cannot have children of the servants telling us how to live our lives. Whoever becomes a stumbling block will be eliminated. We have the power of life and death. Chief Kgoratau had sold out, so his demise was long overdue. We must now install you and announce his passing. Tell me, did you manage to get his royal bead?" King Tau asked.

"Yes, my King. Here it is," Kakata said, handing the royal bead over to King Tau.

King Tau took it and examined it to see if it was genuine. "Yes, it is genuine. I shall call the elders and chief *matwetwe* (head traditional doctor) to come over so that we perform that secret coronation immediately to appease the ancestors before they rise against us," King Tau said.

Kakata was first installed as chief of Motsetona according to secret traditional succession rituals. These

©PJ Ntsoane

were preliminary rituals that preceded public installation where everybody would be allowed to attend. The dead Chief had to be secretly buried by the traditional leaders and doctors. The grave had to be known only by the select few. It had to be done before the death of the king was announced to the tribe. It was their cultural norm that leadership vacuum should not be allowed. Since Chief Kgoratau's first wife had not produced a male heir, Kakata had to succeed him and bear a male successor for Motsetona. He had to take a new bride who was a princess from the royal kraal where Chief Kgoratau had married his first wife. Kakata's old wives had no right to bear an heir to the throne. The heir Princess had to be taken from Kgoratau's first wife's royal kraal to appease her tribe so that they would not think that Motsetona had taken away their position in the royal family.

Kagabo heard about the arrangements of the elders to marry her cousin to come and bear an heir for Motsetona. She regarded that as an insult to her as a person. She decided to oppose the public installation of Kakata as the chief of Motsetona. She declared her intention to succeed her father as the ruler of her people. It was against tradition. Only male children could ascend the throne. Many people were surprised by Kagabo's decision. She contended that she was equally capable of leading her tribe herself as she was not married. She argued that she was educated enough to be an asset to the community as their rightful ruler. Her attempts to convince the elders in the Council of

©PJ Ntsoane

Traditional Leaders about her entitlement were without any success. They didn't want to offend the ancestors by changing their cultural values. However, she got the begging of most women and youth in the area. Malesedi worked day and night to enlighten people about the new direction that had to be taken to correct the imbalances of the past. She campaigned to show the people of Motsetona that Kagabo had the potential and the right to succeed her father. She knew Kagabo from university where she was elected as a secretary and later as the president of the students. Some of those who were led by Kagabo at university were members of the community of Motsetona. Malesedi enlisted the services of those former fellow students to swing public opinion in favour of Kagabo.

Kakata would not go down without a fight. With the backing of King Tau and the local incumbent leaders who had much to lose if Kagabo succeeded, Kakata launched a fierce fight to implement his plan.

King Tau announced a date for the inauguration of Chief Kakata as a successor to the late Chief Kgoratau of Motsetona. As the Paramount King he was the one who had the prerogative to install or remove a chief in his area of jurisdiction. He wanted to preempt the protest planned by Kagabo who was regarded as undesirable and traditionally incapable of taking over from her father. Kagabo resorted to the Constitutional Court on grounds of unfair discrimination on the basis of gender. She also obtained a court interdict against her uncle Kakata. She was determined to win the war for the sake

©PJ Ntsoane

of women in the area and all over the continent of Africa who were denied the same rights accorded their male siblings.

King Tau proceeded with the installation of Kakata as chief according to their plan disregarding the court order. He maintained that he would not allow Western practices to interfere with their African values. On the day of the inauguration there was a hype of activities at Motsetona. The dignitaries included kings, chiefs, political leaders from the provincial and national governments, ambassadors, and CEOs of companies doing business in the area. People were dressed in their traditional regalia. Traditional music groups from surrounding villages had been invited to come and display their musical talents when entertaining those who gathered. African drums were echoing in the escarpment. Kudu horns and reed flutes were bellowing sweet melodies. Ears and eyes of those present were spoilt for variety of beauty and elegance. Twenty bulls were slaughtered to feed those who came. It was one of those festivities that many would witness once in a lifetime. Women competed in ululations.

Paramount King Tau was the main speaker.

"All honourable guests according to your protocol, the press, observers from neighbouring areas and members of the community of Motsetona, I say you are all welcome. I am honoured today to be the one who is tasked with the heavy duty of implementing the work of our ancestors according to our tradition. I knew the late Chief Kgoratau very well. We worked closely together in

©PJ Ntsoane

the development of this area. He was a man of great vision. He was also an incomparable strategist who was a perfectionist when it came to development issues. He was a friend of mine even though he was older. He guided me through many issues that baffled me. Whenever I wanted a solution to a problem he would readily offer his genius. I sometimes forgot that I was the King and delegated crucial issues to him. He always fulfilled his duties without complaint.

Today we are entering a new chapter in the history of this village. Chief Kakata is equally intelligent and dedicated. I have known him for quite a while to say to the people of Motsetona that you are not forsaken with untimely departure of the late Chief Kgoratau. As the second in charge, Chief Kakata always performed crucial duties delegated by the late Chief. In fact he was the first one I ever worked with from this village. We performed several projects together on the economic growth of this area even before I became the King. We were part of the delegation that went to the East to market this area as an investment destination for multi-national companies. Our friends from abroad never disappointed. All is history. Their presence here says volumes. There are many from all over the world who are queuing up for an opportunity to invest in this area. Remember they will only have interest if they see how well we treat our partners in development. People who are in power and who design the policy become the principal determiners of how the world sees us. So far I can say you must thank our ancestors for having given

©PJ Ntsoane

you the leadership you have. Our friends are happy. You can even see by the suits and shoes we are wearing that we have the same taste in fashion." Some people in the audience and members of The Council chuckled.

"Chief Kakata is a great visionary just like his late older brother. He is a man who has an eye for development and market for our natural resources. If it had not been for him many developments in this area would not have been experienced. I have no doubt in my mind that he will bring better changes to this area. We as the Council feel proud and fortunate to have someone like him as a member," he stopped to pick up a leopard skin and a head band made of the tails of a leopard and a hyena which symbolised Motsetona royalty. He looked at the crowd that gathered there. The print and electronic media were clicking their cameras. There were flashlights all over the place. Women were ululating. Kakata was all smiles. He straightened his expensive tie to get ready for proper inauguration. King Tau, accompanied by the chief *matwetwe* (head traditional doctor) walked towards Kakata to perform the inauguration. When he reached Kakata's chieftaincy chair he froze and stared in the distance as if he had seen a ghost. All eyes were on him. People were surprised when he didn't proceed with the inauguration. They slowly followed his eyes to see what he was looking at that seemed to have frightened him. They could not see anything untoward as there were multitudes of people in the yard. It was like everybody was hypnotised as they suddenly became still and quiet.

©PJ Ntsoane

Then there appeared a lonely figure that was pushing through the crowd and moving to the front. It was the white police commander. He headed straight to the stage. He ascended the stage and took out his handcuffs. Everybody wondered who he was going to arrest. He ordered Kakata to stand up and give him his arms as he was arresting him for contempt of a court order and killings of the late Chief Kgoratau and Malesedi's husband. Everybody was aghast at the turn of events. The Commander revealed that they had a solid case as there were witnesses and cameras in the room of the ward where Chief Kgoratau was admitted. Autopsy tests have proved that Chief Kgoratau was murdered. That was not all, the Commander ordered his officers to arrest King Tau and several members of the Council charged with several crimes ranging from murder, attempted murder, common assault, malicious damage to property, fraud, and money laundering. Kagabo was standing with arms folded and beside her were members of the Concerned Women's Club.

"Now the chickens have come home to roost," Kagabo said with a sigh.

"I have long been waiting for this day to see the backs of those *suits*," Malesedi said.

"Now the *suited* are *tied* for real," Kagabo added.

The people broke into song praising Kagabo and Malesedi for ushering in a new chapter in their lives.

The End

©Copyright protected.

©PJ Ntsoane

www.ingramcontent.com/pod-product-compliance
Lightning Source LLC
Chambersburg PA
CBHW060646130626
46555CB00002B/986